"A stag[...] y perfect. It has everything. Exquisite details, world-weary voice, and people worth knowing. It is truly amazing!"

MaryAnne Kolton
Author and Editor of *This Literary Magazine*

"Strong, compelling, raw and human in the best sense. Beautifully written."

Susan Tepper
Author of *Deer and Other Stories*

"Perfect, compact and explosive, closing with the gentlest word."

James Lloyd Davis
Author of *Knitting the Unraveled Sleeves*

"Wow. Beautiful and wonderful and sad and real."

Sally Houtman
Author of *To Grandma's House, We . . . Stay*

"Frighteningly good."

Meg Pokrass
Author of *Bird Envy*

"Superbly explosive. The rage escalates and careens out of control. Amazing."

Ajay Nair
Author of *Desi Rap*

Also by BRETT GARCIA ROSE

Losing Found Things

NOISE

BRETT GARCIA ROSE

NOISE

A NOVEL

BRETT GARCIA ROSE

VELOCITY IMPRINTS

Noise

© 2014 Brett Garcia Rose

All rights reserved. No part of this book may be used or reproduced in any manner whatsoever without written permission except in the case of brief quotations embodied in critical articles and reviews.

Velocity Imprints
contact@velocityimprints.com

Edition ISBNs
Trade Paperback 978-0-9915494-0-5
E-book 978-0-9915494-1-2

First Edition 2014

This edition was prepared for printing by The Editorial Department
www.editorialdepartment.com

cover design by Pete Garceau
Book interior design by Morgana Gallaway

This book is a work of fiction. Names, characters, places, and incidents either are products of the author's imagination or are used fictitiously. Any resemblance to actual events or locales or persons, living or dead, is entirely coincidental.

For Ray

If a lion could talk, we would not hear him.

Ludwig Wittgenstein

THE WORLD IS AN UGLY PLACE, AND I CAN TELL YOU NOW, I FIT IN just fine. You will read what I have written, you will see what I have done, you will judge me and, in the end, you will hate me.

But I write of love.

My name is Leon. This is my story.

Dear Leon:

I know this letter will hurt you, and even as I write it, alone and crying beside our lake, I hope against reason that it will not find you, that it will blow away over the water, floating lost on a pillow of wind to some other place, and that you will go on, wondering; where could she be?

You will imagine me somewhere in Italy or Wales or the South of France with my paintings, and in your dreams you will visit me, as I will you, and we will laugh as we once did, and we will sing and sing and sing, with me as your ears and you as my heart, and we will forever be the children we always wanted to be.

But you deserve to know.

I tried to believe, Leon, I did, with all my strength, and you may yet be right, but there is just not enough time, and too much of everything else. Too much pain, too much failure, too many drugs, too much sadness. There may be places in the world that don't hurt so much, but I can't find them, and I just got tired.

The only thing in this world I'll miss is you. My brother, my quiet little warrior, the one good thing in a world that beat me down. Solve it for me, someday, Leon, conquer the world; tame it for me, as I never could. Your time will come, and you will shine, shine, shine.

Forgive me, Leon, and remember me.
Ever,
Lily

ONE

Present Day

BELOW THE WINDOW, THE GRIND OF TRAFFIC, THE THRUM OF A CITY rush, the weary desperation of people nudged around like house pets. Desolate, gray and quiet. I stand above the big city in a broken building, staring downward at the beginning of my end, remembering.

The leaded glass of the window is layered in patchy grime, swallowed in the corners by a hundred years of paint. The panes resemble dirty soap dishes stacked on end. The air is thick and wet with winter, everything cold to the touch. The room is cell-sized but clean, the clerk before me old and bent and tired.

The sounds I imagine are always sad.

I smile at the clerk and take the metal key from his delicate fingers. He shakes and stoops, emanating a detached, cold kindness. After he leaves I put my backpack on the dresser and the postcard on the desk and then I stand by the window for nearly an hour, watching through the grime as the city crawls beneath me: the glittery maze of Times Square, cars and buses dropped on the sidelines like toys. New York City, dead of winter, everyone feeling punished by lives of their own making. I try to see the noise. I try to come up with a better plan. I try to understand.

My deficit in sound does not enhance my powers of vision in even the smallest of ways. I can only barely remember Lily's face now, a deteriorating photo standing as the only mark in the fog between our times. But I still have the note. Ten years, the corners frayed and yellowed, the ink long since faded. I read it every day, several times on the lonely ones, thousands of times all told, unfolded and folded into pieces by now. She was seventeen then, I fifteen. There was no body. There was no investigation. One policeman, an old family friend, telling us to move on. It was the Deep South. People survive. They overcome. They grit.

I received the postcard two days ago, forwarded through several addresses but eventually finding me, and spent those days driving up in my ancient Ram Charger. I arrived an hour ago. It is not possible for me to be the first to say this, but I'll say it nonetheless: I hate the place. It is cold and ruthless. Humanity in constant battle, all its inhabitants rushing toward some invisible exit, never tiring of the

NOISE

trap. Cities are hell, and New York is the Grand Dame of them all. I have a hard time believing that Lily would ever live in a place like this.

Sweet Lily. Young. Quiet. Hopeful. If there is a picture of kindness anywhere in this place, it wears her face.

After a short nap and a shower, I lock the door of the hotel room and walk three blocks to the diner pictured on the postcard. The sidewalks are narrow and crowded, the pedestrians impartial and unaware of one another in a way that even the simplest of animals are not. They never make eye contact; inches apart, they never touch. A New Yorker approaching another human being is indistinguishable from one approaching a utility pole or a tree.

The Starlight looks like an abandoned trailer that hasn't moved in decades, a broken-down toy of a building, with one side propped up by railroad timbers and electrical wires overhead sagging low enough to touch. There is no parking lot; customers materialize from the surrounding streets, as if drawn by some unknown force.

And they are all frightfully similar to one another. A throwback like this is a study in uniforms. Police, hospital workers, custodians, mail carriers, all served solid, cheap food left over by the former middle class. The kind of place the bulk of Manhattan probably doesn't even notice.

I'm the only one without a name tag. I'm the only one who doesn't belong.

I slide into a small booth against the far wall, my knees hitting the supports underneath the table and shaking the whole thing. The vinyl of the seat bench is cracked, catching on the denim of my pants and hindering my slide to the middle. The air is thick with bacon smoke and the smell of toast.

A young server with limp red hair and *SAM* handwritten on a plastic tag pinned to her chest comes over to the table. She looks bored and vaguely angry. I make the universal sign for coffee with my thumb and index finger and point to an egg platter on the specials page of the laminated menu. Aging crumbs and specks of dirt lie beneath the seared-on plastic, trapped in place, unable to even mold. Bathed in unnatural, too bright fluorescent lights, the entire place feels like one big oven.

Several minutes pass before the server returns with a chipped porcelain cup filled with hot, almost-black coffee. I point to the egg platter again, tapping my finger on the menu to get the server's attention, and then I hold up the postcard toward her face and wait for her to look at it. And she does, briefly, before her eyes dart back to her notepad.

When she finishes writing my order down she glances at the postcard again and shrugs, looking back toward two patrolmen sitting on round stools at the front counter, in front of the cooking area, hunched over plates. I imagine there would be a constant hum to the place, not a noise, exactly, but an aural blanket of sorts, a cushioned bleakness that may or may not be comforting. I wouldn't know.

NOISE

I sip my coffee, reach in my coat pocket for the photo of Lily, and hold it up to her. She takes it in her small hand and shrugs again, dropping the photo on the table as if it's hot, or dirty. I write *Ask?* in my pad and tear off the sheet and slide it to the edge of the table. She leaves the paper on the table and walks away.

She returns a few minutes later with a plate of food. She doesn't say anything about the note. Or if she does, I don't catch it. She has thin lips. Hard to read.

I eat all of the food, suddenly hungry. The last meal I had, sitting in the truck, was at least five hundred miles ago. At the register next to the police officers, a Hispanic guy takes my $20 bill and keeps the change.

"You're looking for Rachael?" he asks. He is overweight and unshaven, with the peculiar habit of avoiding eye contact, his gaze veering toward my right ear.

Lily, I write, and hand the sheet to him.

"Whatever. Last I heard she was at the Ten House. Thanks for the tip," he says, not making eye contact even once. Things like that, the tiny little gestures done or not done, these things speak to the deaf. I stare at the cook while the cop seated across from him stares at me, his head only slightly bigger than my fist. "Women," the cop says, nodding at his coffee cup.

I leave the narrow building with a steady gait, an unreasonable anger trailing behind me. It is an unpleasant feeling I cannot run away from, and I do not try.

TWO

I MOVE THE OLD DODGE TO A COMMUTER LOT IN QUEENS AND walk back over the 59th Street Bridge, wearing my black pea coat, a wool hat and cotton work gloves against the winter wind. It's a long walk, but there is a separate pathway for those without powered vehicles. It's one of those urban designs that would never be included by engineers in the South, where the only people who walk are derelicts and runaway children that no one wants back.

The truck was already old when I bought it back in high school for $500. Stolen, most likely, but I'd done so much work to it that I registered it as a salvage. Regardless of who owned it before, by the time it came into my hands no one would have wanted it, its VIN number older than most of the folks working the DMV. It didn't look like much to begin with and hasn't gotten any prettier, but I've rebuilt the drivetrain from the shaft up. At work I use it to rip tree stumps from the ground. It'll tow six tons. It's big enough to sleep in. I've been told it sounds beautiful.

Lily called it Monster.

At the 13th Precinct in East Midtown, I'm treated courteously and offered a translator to sign for me. The building itself is bigger than my high school back home. A relatively beautiful building, by city standards, at least. I tell Lily's story three times, and with each telling of it I'm shuttled deeper into the station. Hours later I'm sitting in a windowless room with Detectives Jane Reinhart and Rico Santera, seated opposite me at a table bolted to the floor.

If I weren't deaf, I'd never have made it past the lobby.

The walls of the room are concrete, the table dull aluminum, the chairs oak and gouged from years of nerves and restlessness. The translator stands to Jane's right as she reads my story, by now written in my own blocky, practiced handwriting. The female detective is tall and wears no makeup. Her black hair is pulled back in a knot, making her face look serious and angry, but she's easily one of the most beautiful women I've ever seen. Magazine beautiful. Her lips move as she reads in a steady, concentrated rhythm.

Rico is thick-necked and nervous, checking his phone every few seconds. He reminds me of the cheery migrant workers I'd see working in the Deep South, polite people always willing to offer you a hand, but also willing to knife you over a girl or money or simple boredom. The translator stares at me from behind the two detectives, her face bored and severe, her posture correct.

After a few minutes, Jane turns and speaks to the translator, who begins to sign but then stops, waiting for me to look at her.

I don't. In my pad, I write: *Face me so I can understand.* I tear off the sheet and slide it across the table, leaving it on the table in the space between the two detectives. I stare at the detective, not blinking.

Jane sighs, annoyed. "Since it's more than forty-eight hours we can file a missing-persons report, but I have to tell you, there's not much we can do. People come to New York specifically to get lost, and lost they do get." She stares back at me, her gaze penetrating and invasive. This is a different world from the South.

What is Ten House? I write. Jane takes the paper and hands it to Rico. He is short, but powerful, with the ruddy skin of a country Mexican, the kind of person you'd get a drink with, shoot pool. He shrugs and slaps the paper back onto the metal table. "Strip club in Astoria. Dirty place. Ugly girls," he says, smiling broadly. "Lots of crime. Not a place you want to go."

She's a waitress? I write, and shove the paper at him.

Rico shrugs. "They're all waitresses," he says, looking down at the paper but not focusing on it. "Do yourself a favor. Stay away from Ten House. Better yet, go home. We'll keep you informed. You don't need to be here. There's nothing you can do. It's probably not even her."

It's her, I write, and slam the sheet on the surface of the table.

Jane stands and whispers something to the translator that I don't catch and the two of them leave the room. Rico and I sit in silence, which is OK for me, but seems a little awkward for him. He fumbles with his phone the whole time we're alone in the small room, pressing buttons on the glass screen, swiping and tapping and swiping again.

"Listen, Leon," Jane says when she returns, leaning forward and mouthing the words slowly, as if addressing a child. "Ten years is a long time. People change, and New York is a hard place. They do what they need to do."

She tells me to wait, and both of them stand to leave. "We'll be in touch," she says. Rico shakes my hand and wishes me luck, still working his phone.

A few minutes later a uniformed officer comes in with forms for me to sign, after which I'm escorted out of the station and back into the crowded noise of Midtown Manhattan. On the way out, I wonder just what it is that the police of New York City actually do with their time.

THREE

MID-AFTERNOON, AND RAINING. NEW YORK CITY IS THICK WITH black umbrellas and dirty yellow taxicabs and sludge rushing down the streets from the downpour into the sleek, flat drains lining the curbs. Everyone hurrying somewhere, merging with one another on the cold wet streets. Merging, and dismissing, as only urbanites can.

If Ten House is a strip club then it won't be open yet, so I sit in a Starbucks across the street and settle in to watch the diner. I don't imagine Lily will come strolling by for a burger, but it's the only connection I have for now, and there's nowhere else I can think of going.

More police officers and utility workers come and go, a few nurses and EMT personnel from a nearby hospital, and other assorted workers looking for a quick, cheap meal. It's not a place I can picture Lily ever eating in. Her mother raised her with a natural distrust for the cooking of others, especially when done so for money. She'd stop short of calling it poison, but in the rare events that required our presence in a restaurant, the food was carefully inspected. Smelled. Pushed around and turned over with a fork. Held up to the light. This odd relationship with food never transferred successfully onto me, but it had a profound effect on Lily. Bulimia. Anorexia. Depression. Severe weight fluctuations. Frequent, unhealthy bouts of promiscuity.

She'd stare sadly at me whenever I ate, her eyes dark but unflinching. Her mother hardly noticed either of our extremes. To this day my adoption is a profound mystery. Why does a woman who so obviously dislikes children adopt one like me? But in truth I never really knew the woman. She never learned to sign, and, although I learned to read lips, I rarely read hers. Maybe adoptees are simply immune to the adults in their lives.

Lily said my lack of emotion made me a hero to her. I pretended not to understand.

I sip on an espresso and stare at the diner above the rim of the tiny cup. I figure the cook from the diner for a six-to-four shift. I figure he also knows Lily, at least more than he says he does. She always befriended those with the least to offer. Unlike me, she craved people, craved the messy feelings they're so eager to trade. All she ever felt in return was hurt.

NOISE

After several more espressos, I see the cook emerge from the diner, minus the apron but otherwise looking the same as earlier, only more tired. He waddles along with a heavy, awkward gait, wearing a tattered coat and a black baseball cap, looking even more miserable outside in the cold. Whatever anger or emotions I have, deservedly or not, are on him now.

I can never not love Lily.

I follow the cook into a subway station on 41st Street, down a long flight of too-shallow steps and onto the red number seven train that leads back into Queens, nearly losing him in the time it takes to buy a metro card from an automated machine.

I wait inside of the train, one car behind the cook. People crowd around me in silent huffs, settling into the filthy orange seats with their knees pressed tightly together as the doors slide closed. I sweat and fidget in the crowded, overheated space. A policeman's holstered gun rubs against my kidney. A small boy leans against my leg and falls asleep; his mother plays Scrabble on a tablet balanced on bruised knees. Everyone is wet and unhappy, looking to avoid one another with whatever they've got: newspapers, phones, iPods, anything but a reflection of their own tired lives. The train lurches into the dirty dark tunnel and pulls us under the East River.

No one on the train looks at one another. The lights flicker on and off. People wait blankly, as if the train is a time machine, as if the commute itself is some urban form of cryo-sleep, the trip slowly, unknowingly, draining their lives away.

And I realize, in that moment, that there is a constant cost to being in a city like this, slow, steady withdrawals made on your soul. Maybe that's not true of everyone, but it is of me.

We emerge at 74th Street in Jackson Heights, a run-down Hispanic neighborhood just a few miles east of Manhattan, but a different world entirely. Half of the train car exits with me. Outside of the elevated station small boys hawk candy and tax-free cigarettes outside of the station. A lone hooker teeters by on heels, watching me and smiling. Garbage cans and dumpsters overflow with rotting trash, attended by camouflaged homeless pick-ing through them, or sleeping against them. Indifferent policemen sit in their cruisers on the side of the road with the windows up, picking through wrinkled bags of food as if nothing short of open gunfire could budge them. Any one of them could be Rico or Jane, or identical copies, watching me, or not.

I follow about fifty feet behind the cook as he walks north into a housing area, through a cluster of identical red brick buildings all sprouted from the same socioeconomic seed. My longer stride easily keeps the distance between us constant. After a few more blocks, he turns into the walkway of a residential building and I break into a full run, still fast from my high school football days. Just as he's entering the outer door to the building, I plow into his midsection and push him face-first against a concrete wall, hard enough to daze him. I yank his arm behind him and pull until he stops struggling.

The inner lobby is quiet, clean and empty. There's a camera mounted high in a corner with painted-over wires, old and probably just for show.

I punch him in the kidney and find the apartment keys in his front pocket. He is greasy and sweating, on his knees and coughing blood onto the tiled floor. In the reflection of the glass door, I can see his lips and nose bleeding from the impact against the wall. I close my eyes and hold him down by the back of his neck for a few seconds. I think of Jane. And I think of Lily.

I yank him upright and hold him straight against the surface of the glass door. In his ear, I say: "Walk."

The cook crosses the lobby floor toward the elevator, taking halting, unsteady steps and looking back at me over his shoulder. I move my fingers upward in the air, making the sign for stairs. He shrugs and looks back at me every few steps, as if hoping I'll change my mind.

I don't.

We walk up six flights. He curses and pants. The walls are concrete painted dark beige, the floors old industrial linoleum that become less worn as we ascend, damaged areas hammered down where the corners curled. The smell of bleach is strong, hanging in the air like cat urine. The cook stumbles a few times, and each time he falls, I push him further up the stairs.

We emerge on the sixth floor in a narrow hallway. I let him go several feet ahead of me, knowing he won't run. For reasons I've never understood, I've always had a paralyzing effect on people. He motions toward a door at the end of the hallway and I nod, closing the distance and handing him the keys. He unlocks the door and opens it wide. I follow him inside, holding his body directly in front of me as I close the door behind me, and then pulling him against my chest and waiting inside the door. After half a minute, I don't feel any music or other noise, so I let him go.

Inside, the apartment looks like a small one-bedroom. Clean and simple. Smells of soap and dirty laundry and turning fast food and beer and stale cigarette smoke. The place of someone who works a lot and lives little. No paintings or decorations. A tired, sad stop for someone with nowhere else to go. I can imagine a hundred previous tenants living here just like him, in just the same way.

The first door we pass is a small bathroom. I reach into his jacket pocket, find his phone and take it, and then nudge him into the bathroom. As he flushes the toilet and runs the water, I look around the rest of the apartment, but there's not much to see. Few personal belongings. New Yorkers lead sad, solitary lives.

Several minutes later the cook walks into the kitchen and sits at a silver aluminum table sagging at the middle seam;

the kind you find at picnics and fairs and public schools. He offers me a beer as I sit in a chair across from him. I start to write in my pad but he waves at me to stop.

"I told you what I know," he says. His nose is swelling, obviously broken.

Lily, I write.

"Rachael," he says, looking at my face for the first time.

She is my sister. Remember that. I turn the pad to him and he shrugs.

"She's a waitress or something," he says. "I don't know. She comes in after shift sometimes for coffee." He wipes the sweat from his face with a stained dishrag. "I don't know her."

I grab his shirt in one fist and yank him forward onto the table. His chair falls over behind him. The center of the aluminum table bends under his weight. I write: *Where else have you seen her?*

"Fuckin' work, man, I told you. I don't know her."

Ten House? I write.

"Come on, man. I seen her at diner a few times, maybe once or twice at the club. She's always nice to me."

I push him back. He lands hard on the floor, sitting there for several seconds, and then struggles back to his feet, righting the chair behind him and slouching back into it.

What's your name? I write.

"Alex," he says.

Alex, I write. *I need more.*

He shrugs again. "It's a family place," he says. "Small. Mostly regulars."

Ten House, you mean? This is going nowhere. *She's a waitress?*

He shrugs again. I pull him forward again and punch him hard on the nose. More bones crack. Alex doesn't know anything.

When he doesn't respond, I slide the table forward and pin him against the refrigerator in the narrow kitchen.

"It's a family place, man," he says again, his eyes wet.

I need a name, Alex, a boyfriend, something.

He looks at me but says nothing. A full minute passes.

On the counter next to me is a Mac laptop. I take it down and wrap the power cord around it.

Is there a password?

He nods. *No.*

You're loaning this to me to help find my sister. I'll return it when I'm done. I tear off the sheet of paper and leave it on the table.

FOUR

THE ENTRYWAY TO TEN HOUSE IS A WARPED STEEL DOOR AND AN enormous, solitary guard who frisks me and sends me to a teenaged cashier sitting on a high chair behind a wall of thick plate glass. Standard choke-point entry. Without a key, the inner door can only be opened from inside. Once I pay the $10, another guard escorts me up a ramp through what appears to be an elevated neon tube with a suspended, carpeted walkway. When we emerge into the main room, he leads me to a tiny round table next to a stage in the center of the room and waits for a tip.

The wide, booth-type seats are purple velvet, crunchy with stains and dotted with cigarette burns. A bored-looking redhead dances on a small stage, behind an empty moat of sorts, clinging midway up a metal pole and gyrating to music I cannot hear. When she reaches the bottom, she sprays the pole with Windex and disappears into the crowd. I order a beer from a waitress in yellowing Minnie Mouse lingerie. Another girl, more Windex. Other men surround me discreetly, looking but also not looking. The lighting, subdued and constant, relaxes me.

Every song brings another naked woman into my field of view to linger until I pay them a dollar and they move on to the next patron. Outside, in the real world, my size alone would scare them, but not here. Here, the woman is the weapon. Backed by at least twelve hundred pounds of security.

I don't see Lily. I don't see Rachael. She may have changed, more than just her name; she might be so physically different now that I would not even recognize her if I did see her. She may have blonde hair and green contacts. A crew cut, extensions, curls, flat iron. She could be anyone. I put her photo down on the table in front of my beer. Next to the photo, I lay down a $20 bill. If a girl looks at the photo and takes the bill, I figure they know her. Maybe.

I feel the music in my feet, in my ass, in my scalp. The entire room pulses with a tired, persistent energy, a timeless, dreamless space. An hour. Three beers. Neon lights. Speakers the size of refrigerators. No one stops. No one looks at the photo. In the mirror behind the stage, all I see is my own tired face looking back at me.

Just as I decide to leave the weight shifts on the velvet

couch to my right and I turn around, coming face to face with a young brunette, maybe mid-twenties, with a sinewy body and sharp, bright blue eyes. She puts her hand on my arm and leans into me, her lips nearly touching mine. "Do you want to go to a private room for a dance?" she asks. When I shake my head, she taps her thumb against my arm and extends her index finger toward the photo, not taking her eyes off mine. "Are you sure?"

I nod OK and she takes the $20 bill off the table and leads me by the hand through a dimly lit hallway and into a VIP section lined with small, curtained rooms. No one watches us. Inside, she nudges a round table aside with her foot, sits me down on a couch identical to the one outside and arranges herself sideways on my lap, facing me.

"Elle used to read lips," she says. "It was a trick she'd do from behind the two-way mirrors in the VIP rooms where we'd film. That's her, right?" She holds the photo toward a candle perched on a ledge behind the couch. "She's so young there . . . same eyes, though." She's close enough for me to feel her breath on my cheek as she speaks, to feel the vibration of her voice. But there is none. She's just mouthing the words.

I nod.

"She learned it from you?" she asks.

"Learned what from me?" I say, using my real voice now.

"To read lips."

"No," I say. "She taught it to me. Her name is Lily."

"Whatever," she says. "We all have names."

The music pounds through the walls in a vibratory assault just for me. I glance around for the cameras I'm sure exist, but they're well hidden.

"You're the brother. I saw a photo. I sent the postcard," she says, looking down at my chest.

"Where is she?"

"That's it. Elle—Lily—told me to mail it if anything happened. Something happened."

I wait for her to continue. When she looks up, a single tear runs down her cheek and lands on my leg. "What happened"? I ask.

"I told you . . . they film. Everything. They're filming us right now," she says, again just mouthing the words.

"The postcard. Why that diner? Who is there?"

"I don't know."

"She was a dancer here?"

The girl leans away and looks at me, stunned. "What? No, she doesn't work here. She's married to the owner's son. Hung around here sometimes, tried to get to know us. She was this lonely, quiet woman, just wanted to be around us, I think."

"Lily's married?" For some reason, her being married has never occurred to me. It seems wrong, odd, as if someone has stolen part of her.

She nods. "They live downtown somewhere. Not sure where."

NOISE

"What's his name?"

"Victor."

Just as I'm about to ask the girl who the owner is, a hand reaches around the curtain and yanks the girl backward over the couch, jerking her out of the room by her hair like a doll. Seconds later the hand comes back, parting the curtain with an H&K Mark 23 Tactical, a .45 caliber handgun with a matte finish favored by Navy SEALs. A beautiful $2,500 weapon, held steady in a hand the size of a Frisbee and aimed at my left eye. It's like staring into a tunnel.

"I like to greet my new customers," says a second, smaller man, walking around the first and sitting gingerly on the velvet couch next to me, close enough that our legs touch. He is dressed in a thin polyester suit, pale gray and shiny, something I'd imagine would be more at home in Miami than here. His face is frail and twitchy, with greasy blond hair and the soft, darkened teeth of a meth-head, the kind of guy you can kill with a single punch. I lean forward and gesture at my notepad on the table. The gun follows my hand. The second man nods, his goatee dipping toward the small, round table.

I'M DEAF, I write, in big block letters, filling the entire page and holding the notepad up in front of him. His eyes go wide in a sort of mock amusement, laughing as he stands up from the couch and slaps me on the shoulder. The first guy lowers his gun, the large weapon disappearing into a cross-shoulder holster.

"You like my girls, eh?" the smaller man says. I shrug. He stops laughing. "Guy as big as you, asking questions, makes people nervous, I suppose. Tell my guys, better safe than sorry, eh? Paranoid fuckers, I say. Tough business. Shit neighborhood."

He walks partway out, and then leans back and peeks around the curtain so that only his head is visible. "Shot at the bar, my friend. No pun intended." They both start laughing. He stares at me for a few seconds longer, the smile gone, and then snaps his head forward and disappears down the hallway.

I finish my beer and follow the same hallway back into the main room. I wait at the bar for another hour, looking around the room for the brunette, but she doesn't return. The guy with the gun stands on a small set of stairs on the other side of the stage, maybe forty feet away. The girl, I realize, said nothing about the photo.

FIVE

I LEAVE THROUGH THE FRONT DOOR AND WALK SEVERAL SHORT blocks back to the truck. I drive around the corner and up an adjacent alley until I can see the back door of the club, then I back the truck next to a dumpster and shut off the engine.

Hours tick by and I start to wonder if I'm wrong about the back door, if they all just spill out of the front after closing.

Shortly after 2 a.m. the steel door opens. Several girls come out, escorted by the same man who held the gun inside. After three trips to the parking lot with girls I don't recognize, the man emerges with the brunette from the private room, guiding her by the elbow as she stumbles along the cracked pavement. I'm directly across from them, maybe twenty feet away, and slip out of the truck silently, having disabled the interior light years ago. He's walking slowly, at her speed, probably accompanying her to the subway station. I make up the distance in around five seconds.

When I'm within three feet, I lean forward in my stride, my right fist following my left leg, hitting the back of his neck with my fist while my right foot is still in the air. Superman Punch, we called it in training, the power of the strike multiplied by the momentum of the stride and gravity itself. Dealing with a neck that size I need all the help I can get. He falls to the pavement face first and doesn't move. I ignore the girl's screams and kneel down, rolling the man's body over and retrieving his wallet, gun, keys, money, phone and some papers from his jacket pocket. Nothing else.

You wanted to help me, I write in my pad and hand the sheet to the girl. Then I say the words: "So help."

She looks down at the body on the pavement. Her hands shake when she tries to pull her jacket tighter around her chest. "They're going to kill you," she says.

In my pad, I write *Lily,* and hand the sheet to her. I walk back toward the Dodge. The girl hesitates, but follows a few seconds later.

We drive for several miles before pulling into a driveway and parking on the side of a gas station deep in Astoria. The girl waits in the passenger seat as I go into the station and return minutes later with two coffees. I hand one to her and open the cover of mine, blowing on the surface to dissipate the heat.

The big engine in the front rumbles in the seats and floor.

NOISE

A light rain pebbles the windshield. When I start to write again she puts her hand on mine, pulling my chin toward her with the other hand.

"My name is Sara," she says.

"Leon," I answer back, careful not to scare her even more with my voice. "Where's Lily?"

She shrugs, a little-girl gesture like Lily used to do when she was frustrated, when she was younger.

"OK," I say. "Her husband?"

"Works on Wall Street, some kind of finance guy. He's involved with the club somehow, but he doesn't work there. Comes in from time to time looking for her and they fight. Always wearing a suit. Always fidgeting and looking uncomfortable. Doesn't want her there, I guess. Doesn't even want to be there himself," she says.

"Who's the other guy, the skinny one in the club?"

"Listen, I have to get my kid to school in a few hours and then go to work. I can't really help you. I'm already in trouble, I think."

"You work in the morning?" I say.

"I work in a vet's office," she says. "I really need to go."

She reaches for the door handle, and I grab her arm to hold her back. She pulls her arm free but doesn't leave, instead leaning her head against the cracked dashboard. After a minute I realize she's crying.

She turns back to me slowly, her face red and streaked, trails of mascara disappearing underneath her chin.

"Was she kind to you?" I say.

She doesn't answer right away. A light rain falls on the windshield of the Dodge, transforming the view of the gas station into a cheap Impressionist painting but also enhancing Sara's beauty somehow, the small round shadows mottling her skin and making her seem more primal, sad and soulful in a way she hadn't seemed just minutes before.

"She talked about you a lot," she says. "Idolized you, I think. This mythical, ageless brother. Everyone who knew her wanted one. Said you got in trouble a lot, though."

"Sara," I say again. "I need to find her."

"I think she's dead, Leon." Sara's lips barely move. "I think she killed herself."

The air in the truck grows thinner, colder. "Why? You don't know that."

"I would if it happened to me."

"If what happened?"

The rain starts to fall harder now, collecting in a small flood surrounding the Dodge, marooning us in the ancient truck. I pull Sara's chin toward me, inches from my face. "What happened?"

Sara stares back for a moment, defiant, and then answers, slowly mouthing each word. "They filmed her, I said. They raped her, and they filmed her."

The rain slows to a drizzle. I shut the ignition on the Dodge. The engine rumbles and the truck shudders for a few seconds, holding on, and then goes still.

"Who, Sara?"

She looks away from me, facing the side window again. I pull gently on her chin, so I can see her lips.

"I think they were afraid of the police. Something was going on, she was talking to the cops, or having an affair, or something. I don't know." She runs her hands along her cheeks and pins her hair behind both ears. "I was there the night they took her in the office. I heard her screams, but I thought they were just beating her. A few hours later she came out of the office wearing just a shirt, no pants or shoes."

Sara turns toward the windshield once more. I can't hear her voice, but I get the feeling she's speaking very softly. I touch her arm with my fingers and she turns back to face me. "She was bleeding from her face and down her legs," she says, continuing as if she hadn't stopped. "Bleeding so much that her feet kept slipping as she walked, but she didn't even seem to notice. It was horrible, like she was sleepwalking, and she had this lost, vacant look in her eyes. She kept stumbling, falling onto tables and rolling over onto the floor, then getting up on her hands and knees, pulling herself upright and trying to walk in the same direction. No one looked at her. No one helped. Rastov, the manager, he had this crazy, wide-eyed look. The Bear just laughed. The other brother, Victor—her husband—looked pretty sick, like he was gonna vomit. Elle just walked right past them and out the door, dazed, as if they weren't even there. That was around a week ago. She never came back."

"The Bear?"

"Rastov's father. Izgoi or something like that. Everyone just calls him Bear, or The Bear. He owns the place. That same night, he brought those of us who saw her walk out of the office, brought us into a room in the basement with a small TV and showed us the video. Said none of us could talk to the police, or to anyone. Said we're all filmed, all of the time. Scared the shit out of me. All of us. It was the worst thing I'd ever seen. She just kept screaming, even when she lost her voice, when there was no sound left, she was still trying to scream. Rastov keeps some of her fingernails in the desk too, I think, the ones that tore out that night. There were bloody handprints everywhere."

"The film," I say, facing the windshield again. "Where's the film, Sara?"

"I don't know. There's a wall safe in the office upstairs at the club, maybe there. But really I don't know."

When I don't respond she pulls my chin back to her.

"I'm sorry, Leon. I really am sorry."

"Me too," I say.

SIX

BY THE TIME I DROP SARA AT HER PLACE DEEP IN BROOKLYN, AND the Dodge back in Queens, it's nearly 4 a.m. Sara texted me after I dropped her off, asking if I want to meet after her shift at the vet's office, but I have no idea if she'll show. The Home Depot in Astoria doesn't open until 6 a.m., so I go to the hotel to shower, and then back to the Stardust for breakfast.

Alex, the cook, is back at the counter when I arrive, but ducks into the kitchen when he sees me. His face is bruised and deep purple, with a strip of first-aid tape across the bridge of his nose. The waitress is the same redheaded girl as the previous day. The food is bland, but hot. I linger for a while, drinking four cups of coffee and making lists.

At 6 a.m. I take the subway to a Home Depot in Astoria and use my credit card to pick up the largest sledgehammer and fire ax they have, a smaller, one-handed drilling sledge, a 23-ounce claw hammer, a four-foot pry bar, some duct tape, 3/8-inch cable ties and a six-gallon gas jug. Back by the register, I pick up a small collapsible hand truck in case the safe is small enough to take to the truck and strong enough to withstand the hammers.

I linger in the aisles for a while longer, picking up a new flashlight, batteries and some smaller items I think I might need, and then I walk three miles back to the truck. I stow the gear in the back of the truck with my other tools, cover the pile with a work blanket, and by 8 a.m. I'm back at the hotel. When sleep comes, it comes hard.

When I first met Lily, I was nine, and she was eleven. Her schooling was more advanced than mine, which, by Western standards at least, was pretty much nonexistent. We'd had one class in the orphanage every Sunday, and the only other time we'd be allowed in the building was when a white woman or a couple came to look at us. Lily's mom was at least the twentieth I met. Everyone wants the babies. The rest of us are just too fucked up.

Aside from class and the adoption line, we lived on the streets of Nigeria, like a lot of the population. We drifted the alleys and shanties, not old enough or strong enough to claim any one space. We'd beg for money. We'd steal. We'd fight for survival or entertainment. Shoot. Knife. Run. We'd work as makeshift guards or as couriers or bait. It didn't matter to us. We had rifles when the rest of the world had toys. If we got too sick to keep moving, someone would drag us into the shadows, next to a dumpster or a warehouse or an abandoned car. They would cover us with a blanket, kiss us on the forehead and we would die.

I had no interest in leaving my Nigeria, even though the thought of flying in a plane fascinated me. It was my home. I understood it, and I understood my place there. I was nowhere near the top back home, but nor would I ever be on the bottom, like I am here in America. However bad it got for me, it could always be worse. I was young, smart and stronger than most.

The idea of growing up is a foreign concept invented by Westerners to slow everything down. Whatever age we were in Africa, we were already grown up, already as old as we were likely to get. By the time I was seven, I'd lost count of the people I'd knifed. By the time I left Africa, at nine, I was as hard as a child could become in any country and still remain free.

When Lily gave me her bed on my first night in America, it was the first time I ever laid on a real mattress, the kind with springs, and the first time the mosquitoes couldn't get at me. And when I couldn't sleep for fear of falling off the edge of the raised bed, Lily dragged the mattress onto the floor and sat with me, arranging her dolls around my arms and legs and murmuring to herself. I always slept easily;

we took it wherever and whenever we could, but never as peaceful as on that first, foreign night.

From the moment I met Lily, she'd made me feel safe somehow, her presence slowing the world for me, allowing me to watch a little instead of always running. She was the first kind person I'd ever met. And the last.

When I awaken in the hotel bed, it's already dark. I've slept the entire day. I'd planned to try to locate some blueprints of the building where Ten House is located, but it's not critical. As far as I could tell, there were only exterior alarms, which I wouldn't be tripping until the way out anyway. If they even worked at all.

SEVEN

SARA TEXTS ME LATE IN THE AFTERNOON, SENDING AN ADDRESS IN Brooklyn for us to meet. I take the subway back to the truck, and then drive around the Belt Parkway and deep into Brooklyn. When I arrive at the address, I discover it's a small Thai restaurant. Sara waits in a booth against the wall in the back. She wears a simple black dress.

"Is this a date?" I slip into the bench seat across from her.

"Strippers don't date," she says.

"I don't know anything about Thai food," I say, looking at her. She's even more beautiful than she was the previous night.

"I ordered when I saw your truck. I can't believe people still drive those things."

"Why not?"

She brushes her bangs away from her eye with her fingers, trying unsuccessfully to trap them behind her ear. "Hello? Global warming? Don't you watch the news?"

"It's cheap," I say. She looks sophisticated, professional. More like an attorney than a stripper.

"Not for the rest of the planet."

"I'm not from here, Sara," I say. "Climate change started for us centuries ago. Much of Africa used to be a rain forest. It wasn't cars or coal or hairspray or cow farts. It was just bad luck, chunks of the earth floating around."

"So you don't believe it was caused by humans?" She's visibly angry.

"I do believe. I just don't care."

"We're destroying the earth, with our cars and our planes and our factories." She stirs a red drink in a tall, curved glass.

"The earth will survive," I say. "We're just destroying ourselves, and I'm not a big fan of humanity."

"I hope you like Thai beer," she says, frowning.

I take a long sip from the brown bottle. "It'll do. Tell me about Lily."

"I don't know her well. Only saw her maybe ten or fifteen times. But I liked her," she says. "Where do you live?"

"In my truck, mostly. I clear construction sites, move around a lot. The truck makes more sense than an apartment."

She stares at me, ignoring the waiter as he places the food on the table. "It sounds lonely," she says. "It sounds like Lily."

"She was always lonely," I say. "Sensitive in a way that I

wasn't. She tried to teach me to cry many times. It never worked. Well, it worked once, with onions and pepper involved."

"Other family?"

"I'm adopted."

"Obviously."

"Her mother died less than a year after," I say. "She never recovered after Lily disappeared."

"And you?"

"Me what?"

"Have you recovered?"

I consider the question for several seconds, but there's really no answer. "I don't need to recover," I say. "I was always alone. You would have liked her mother, though. Climate change, adoption, education, homelessness, world hunger, you name it, she was on it."

"But not for you, I take it. Or for Lily."

"Americans and their causes," I say.

Sara digs into her food, momentarily forgetting me. We eat the rest of the meal in silence. Aside from Lily and her mother, this is the longest I've ever spent alone with a woman. I don't want it to end.

"How much do you understand?" Sara asks, after the waiter clears the plates and takes an order for dessert and coffee.

"Understand what?" I say.

"Lip-reading."

"It varies from person to person," I say. "Usually at least half of the words. It's the same theory as speed-reading, but we get to fill in the blanks contextually. Body language, mostly, so we have an advantage."

"Half the time," she says. "You're wrong pretty often then."

"Not wrong," I say. "Incorrect."

"There's a difference?" she asks.

"There's a difference."

She continues talking but the waiter returns, blocking my view with his arm. He brings two small dishes of tea-flavored ice cream and two mugs of steaming black coffee.

Sara smiles and eats her dessert slowly, clearly a fan of sweets. Mine is gone in three bites.

"You're very black." She sips her coffee. "I mean, even for a black person, you're very black."

"How do you know Lily was lonely?"

"Because she was always alone. The only times she ever smiled were the times she'd talk about you. It was such a stark difference that most of us just thought you were a fantasy she'd created, a made-up fact of a faraway happiness. People do that, you know. I still can't believe you're a real person."

"She wasn't happy back then, either."

"Yes, Leon. She was. You're wrong more often than you'd like to think."

"Maybe," I say.

"You think she's still alive?"

"I *assume* she's still alive, and I act on that assumption."

"You're very defensive when it comes to language, you know that? Wrong, incorrect, assume, think; it's all the same shit when you get right down to it, isn't it?"

"Yes." I stare at my coffee. "I suppose it is."

"You assume she's alive so you can search for her and justify hurting whoever gets in your way. If you thought she was dead, then you'd just be punishing people. Revenge. Classic shadow thinking."

"Shadow thinking?"

"Jung," she says, finishing her coffee.

I smile at her. "Stripper school?"

"Asshole. B.S. in psych, Amherst. But you're right, it's all bullshit. We can only explain behavior after it happens, and we do that by selecting a narrow set of facts from a near-infinite pool of observation. You could say you are here, in this place, at this particular time, because it is raining, and find abundant factual support for that theory."

"But you'd be incorrect."

"No," she says. "You'd be *wrong*."

"You could have been a lawyer." I count out $28 for the meal and the tip.

"I could have been a lot of things."

"You're a mother," I say. "The most important job anyone can have."

"This coming from an orphan?"

As we're walking toward the door, I see her face in the

reflection of the glass. She wipes away tears with the sleeve of her sleek jacket. We walk to the truck in silence.

"Lily was going to search the world for places that didn't hurt," I say, driving back across Brooklyn and toward Queens.

"What does that mean?"

"It was like her religion," I say. "Some faraway place where she would be happy, where life would make sense. She talked about it all the time."

I reach into my inside pocket and pull out the taped-together note Lily tacked to the pier by our lake so many years ago and hand it to Sara. "This is the last I'd ever heard from her."

She reads the note in silence. After several minutes, I realize she's reading it over and over again.

"It sounds just like her. Maybe she should have died, back then, but I think she just wanted to make one grand push, without the responsibility of failure, which she obviously expected. I think she couldn't bear the thought of disappointing you."

Inside the truck, I say nothing, pulling around to the back entrance of Ten House. When I stop, Sara pulls my chin toward her face and kisses me on the lips. Not a romantic, sexual act, but a hungry, desperate kiss, holding her lips still against mine for nearly a minute, and then pressing her forehead against mine before slowly pushing me away and smiling.

NOISE

"I know you don't believe it, Leon, but I think you're a good man." She gets out and closes the door of the truck. Through the glass, I see her last words. "I really do."

I remain frozen in my seat, watching as she disappears into the doorway of Ten House, and I don't move for several minutes, just staring at the door. After a while I put the truck in gear and drive away slowly, thinking how glad I am that Lily had had someone like Sara in her life, and how differently it might have turned out if they had been sisters. If I'd stayed in Africa.

And, as I drive out of the parking lot, I have one last thought, and it saddens me. I stop at the first red light, shaking my head, and I say aloud, watching my lips move in the rearview mirror: "No, Sara. You're wrong about me."

EIGHT

I DRIVE AROUND QUEENS FOR SEVERAL HOURS BEFORE RETURN-ing to Astoria and parking the truck in another commuter lot underneath the elevated subway, the yellow N/R line, a few blocks from the back of the club. At 11 p.m. I walk to the back door and clip the power line to the exterior light with cutters from my toolbox, and go back to the Dodge to wait.

At 1:45 a.m. I walk to the back of Ten House again and wait around the corner of the building, on the opposite side of the parking lot and in view of the rear door. The first girl comes out at 2:15 a.m., escorted by the same man who held the gun on me. Sara comes out a few minutes later, leaning against the same man and laughing as she teeters along the pavement in five-inch heels.

Over the next twenty minutes, the man walks two more girls out, then two groups of two and three walk themselves out. I counted five girls last night, plus a waitress, a bartender and I assume two or three more working the private rooms. When the next girl comes out, once again escorted by the same man, I sling my duffel bag over my shoulder and make a run for the door, catching the edge just before it closes.

I walk in on the first floor of the club, past stacks of boxes, then past several doors opening to dark rooms, mostly empty, before reaching a locked utility closet at the end of the hallway. I open the lock with my knife and slip inside to wait. Like at most other clubs, the cleaning and maintenance crew, if any, won't show up until daylight, at least 6 a.m., when wages return to day rates.

I feel the footsteps of the big man once more as he walks down the hallway and out the door an hour later, and then nothing.

At 4:40 a.m. I stand from the box I'd been sitting on, stretching to my full height and trying to work the kinks from my back. I exit the closet and walk down the hallway, shielding my flashlight with my hand so I can just barely see my feet, and walk up the stairs to the main room. A place like this wouldn't have guard dogs due to allergies, smells and noise, and it's probably not profitable enough to hire a night guard. Besides, it's a strip club. The valuables drive themselves home every night after shift.

NOISE

From the height and shape of the building I could tell from the outside that there was a small third floor, but it takes me a while to find the stairwell. I search the entire second floor before locating a flush, featureless, padlocked door at the end of the VIP section. I use the long pry bar and head up the stairs.

I figure I'm safe now. If the manager were living here he'd be upstairs, and could not have padlocked the door from the outside. At the top of the stairs is a short hallway with three doors, one on each side and one at the end. I check each one with the flashlight. Bathroom, closet, office.

I go through the drawers and files in the office, packing anything that looks interesting into my duffel bag and looking for a combination written down somewhere. I lie underneath the desk, shining my light upward and sideways, but as far as I can tell, it's just a regular desk, no hidden compartments, and no combinations written anywhere. Plan A, killed.

I locate the safe easily enough, mounted in the wall behind an awful painting of a horse. I'd hoped it would be a fire safe, the kind used more for document protection than burglary. They often look the same, but are different. Plan B, killed.

It's a burglary safe, all right, but an old one, the mechanical sort with a single dial. These can be easily cracked by people with good hearing, but they also tended to be front-fortified, meaning most of the work went into the doors and hinges. Since they were designed to be permanently installed, a certain amount of ingenuity is assumed on the part of the person installing it. Shoving one into a wooden wall and surrounding it with sheetrock and a pretty molding is almost as good as leaving the written combination in a drawer.

I swing the long ax sideways at the wall beneath the safe, taking out the wooden molding, then the decorative sheetrock, then the frame of four-by-fours that comprise the homemade mount. After a dozen swings, the safe falls to the floor, shaking the floorboards of the office.

I once saw a man break into an office building back home to get at a tall, free-standing gun safe in the corner of a conference room. I was six at the time, but could already handle an AK-47. The other kids were secretly taking bets on how he would get the thing opened, but instead of trying to open it right there he placed a dolly next to the safe and pushed it over, letting it fall sideways onto the wheeled platform. Three office workers were tied up in the bathroom, one already dead. There was dust everywhere.

One of the kids got impatient and asked the man how he planned to open the safe, knowing there were not enough of us to carry it down all of the stairs we came up through. The man smiled and said, "I don't have to open it. If God wants us to have the guns, he'll open it himself." He called us over, and we all got behind the dolly and pushed it as fast as we could down the straight hallway, into an office at the end, and right through the sheetrock of the outside wall. The safe fell twenty stories to the street below. God, it turned out, wanted it to be opened after all.

I slide the desk away from the rubble and turn the safe over, tapping each wall with the claw hammer and holding my fingers against the metal surface. The sides are rock solid, the vibrations from top and bottom feel a little longer, so I figure it probably only locks to the left, with hinges sunk through the corners on the right. The back is a little softer, probably walled and plated. I slide the safe to the middle of the room and turn it on its face.

Using the ax again, I take slow, full swings, each turn dimpling the metal inward until there's a slit about twice as wide as the ax blade. I stand on the corners of the safe, insert the curved end of the long pry bar into the slit, and lay all my weight on it, bouncing on the flexing bar. The slit bends open slightly to resemble a fish mouth.

I shine my light inside and see some papers and a small orange-and-silver hard drive, around four inches long, too big to fit through the opening. I go back to the ax and start to work on a crosswise slit, then go back to the pry bar.

After two more cycles of this facing in different directions there are four identical slits on the back wall of the safe. I turn the safe on its side to shift the contents, and then turn it back on its face, going to work with the big sledgehammer. After eleven swings, one side of the weakened back caves in, breaking the thin internal shelf. I reach inside, take the hard drive and papers and wipe my prints from the safe and desk. My sweat is everywhere, but I don't think it matters much. Unless a rich white kid is kidnapped, DNA is just too expensive to chase. Besides, my DNA has no record. I don't even have a birth certificate.

On the way out of the basement hallway I find the room with the video equipment Sara described to me and smash it with the sledgehammer into a long, flat pile.

NINE

SIX A.M. THE SUN IS ALREADY BREAKING. I DROP THE DODGE IN the original lot in Queens and go back to the hotel to get the laptop I borrowed from the cook.

I connect the portable hard drive and go through the folders. There are hundreds of scanned documents, along with some Word and Excel files. Further down, in another folder, I find the videos and start viewing the numbered files, one by one. Even without the sound, the images are easily the worst things I've ever seen. Lily is number seventeen. Her hair is dark and curly, not blonde as she was back in South Carolina, and she's much thinner than I remember, gaunt and bony.

I can barely stand to see her naked, much less like this, but I force myself to watch every frame. I watch the file straight through several times, memorizing the faces. The Bear. The manager. The man with the gun. Another tall man in a suit, probably the husband, watching from the side. One more guy I've never seen. The office is clear but nothing else stands out.

I watch Lily scream, cry, punch and kick and scratch, trying anything to get away. Toward the end, when the men are spent and finished, they throw her through the air, across the room, her body slamming against a wall in the corner and crashing to the floor in a heap. The camera zooms in for some last closeups, then the operator sets the camera back on the tripod, and the men leave the room.

Lily lies on the floor for twenty minutes, curled into a fetal position and hugging her knees to her chest, tears flowing from her eyes and blood from her mouth and legs, but I've never seen her so defiant. So beaten, yet so strong. Right there, watching her watch the camera, I realize that there are no limits to love, no limits to cruelty, to punishment. To revenge.

Finally, she gets up and walks on shaky legs toward the camera, staring into the lens as she passes out of view of the camera, and then the screen rushes toward the wall, as if the camera was thrown across the room. I move the slider backward and stare at each man's face again, and realize one more thing: I don't want to find Lily. I want to find *them*. And that scares me a lot less than it should.

I close the file and reopen it in the iMovie software that

came with the Mac. After reading through the online help, I learn how to isolate and capture still images of the faces. Once I finish, I close the software, e-mail the images and the video to my Gmail account and erase the files from the Mac.

I double-click the QuickTime movie icon on the desktop once more to get back to the original file from the hard drive, and that's when I see the copy. *Copy of 17.mov* was last accessed three days ago.

TEN

AT 8 P.M. I TAKE THE RED NUMBER SEVEN TRAIN BACK TO JACKSON Heights and wait at the cook's building until I see some drunk teenagers walking in. I follow them inside, ascending the six flights once more, slowing toward the end.

Alex opens the door wide after the second knock and I rush inside, swinging the laptop against his already swollen face so hard that the aluminum frame bends and the screen shatters. I shut the door behind me and slam the machine against his head several more times until it's just pieces. Then I drag him by his hair into the kitchen.

In the kitchen, I find duct tape and secure him to the chair. He's nearly unconscious at this point, so I grab a two-liter bottle of Coke from the refrigerator and pour the contents over his head and face.

On my pad, I write: *Tell me about the video. If you lie, I'll kill you.*

Alex spits off to the side, blood trickling down his lips. He sighs and talks slowly. "She . . . Rachael . . . she gave that to me and said to give it to her brother if he ever showed at the diner, and to the cops if he didn't."

I did show up.

"Too late, man. So did that freak Rastov, from the club, and his hairy father. They're scary fuckers, OK? Asked me if I'd ever seen her in the diner with some guy. I said no but they didn't believe me."

What guy? I write.

Alex shrugs. "I'm telling you what I know."

What does the diner have to do with the club?

"Dunno."

In my own voice, I say: "How many times did you watch the video?"

Alex jerks slightly, sinking against the back of his chair, reacting to either the question or the sound of my voice itself.

I leap up and swipe the metal table aside. He screams as I grab him by the ears and twist them toward his chin. Then I lower my right hand to his crotch and squeeze his testicles until they just about burst.

"How many times have you watched the video, Alex?"

He doesn't answer, so I squeeze harder. "Who was the fifth guy?"

NOISE

"What?"

"The fifth guy in the video, the guy in the diner, same guy?" I say.

When he doesn't answer, I grab a steak knife from the muck in the kitchen sink and drive it into his thigh, twisting it at the end and covering his mouth so he can't scream.

"Same guy, Alex?"

He nods, shaking and crying.

"Who is he?"

I cover his mouth again and pull out the knife, ready to do the same to the other leg as he starts squirming and mumbling against my hand. I stop and remove my hand so I can see his lips. The swelling is much worse now, making it harder to understand him clearly.

"Cop," he says. "Fifth guy . . . a cop."

"And the suit?" I'm certain that it's the husband.

"Don't know, man." His eyes are pleading. "I swear it."

I hold the knife blade against his neck, my arm outstretched to put some distance between us.

"Please," he says. "It's all I know. I wanted to help her, but I was scared. She was my friend."

I hold the blade of the knife against his neck for a few seconds longer, staring at his ruined face. For the first time, his eyes meet mine.

I place the knife in his right hand and walk out of the apartment.

ELEVEN

ON THE SUBWAY, I SEND A TEXT MESSAGE TO THE DETECTIVE, JANE, saying I have information and asking her if she can meet. We agree on a diner near the Midtown East precinct, where we first met.

Bring a laptop, I write, just before the train dips under the East River and my phone loses its signal.

Forty-five minutes later, we're sitting side by side in a booth in the far corner of a diner much larger and much nicer than the Stardust, far enough away from the other customers that presumably they can't hear. As we're huddled over the laptop watching the video I write *Rastov, Bear, Bouncer, Husband/Son? Cop?* I tap Jane on the arm and point to the words and the figures on the screen.

Jane ignores me, keeping her eyes on the screen. At the

end of the video, she sips her coffee and purses her lips. Her face is ash-white, angry, her black hair pulled into a bun behind her head.

"Where did you get this?"

"A cook from a diner . . . friend of Lily's, I think," I say. "It was shot in the office of Ten House."

She finishes her coffee and starts the video over, stopping several times, pointing to the words written in my pad and the figures on the screen, like I did moments before.

"Rastov. The Bear . . . Aslan Izgoi. The bouncer . . . Rastov's bestie. Associated since grade school, apparently. The husband, Victor Izgoi, Rastov's brother. Wall Street guy, legit but handles the books for The Bear, washing at least some of the cash. Keeps it in the family," she says. When she reaches the fifth guy she pauses again and looks at me.

She takes my pad and writes slowly: *CI-14554764. Lily.*

"She was a confidential informant," she says. "I'm sorry, Leon. I couldn't tell you."

"Where is she?" I yell, the words tearing in my chest. People stop eating and stare at our table.

"The cop," Jane says, straining to keep her voice low and steady. "Wife and three little girls." She points back at the laptop, moving the slider back and then pressing the arrow key to advance the video frame by frame. She stops as the man's naked body covers Lily, and then, using the same key, advances the video to a part where he is pulled off her. She presses the pause key, freezing the video. "See the blood?

He's already been shot," she says. "They were probably trying to force him to have sex with her but I doubt he could even if he'd wanted to. Two nine-mils in the abdomen. You die slowly, and very painfully."

"He's dead?" I say.

"He's dead." She's still looking at the screen.

"Is Lily dead?"

"I don't know, Leon. Truly," she says. "I need to talk to this guy, the cook. Where is he?"

"Why haven't you arrested them?"

She doesn't answer.

I look down at my watch. "Check the hospitals closest to Jackson Heights, Queens. Alex something. Works at the Stardust diner in Times Square. He'll be checking in soon," I say. "Various injuries."

"Be careful, Leon," she says. "You have to deal with us, too, you know."

As I stand up to leave, I tell her to check her e-mail later tonight, before she goes to bed.

"I don't go to bed," she says.

I walk fifteen blocks back to the hotel to retrieve the hard drive, and then rent a computer at an Internet café a few blocks away from the hotel. I upload all of the video files on the hard drive to Jane's e-mail, hoping that police accounts do not come with size limits.

It takes around three hours. When the upload completes I print out the rest of the files for myself, and then log into my

Gmail account and print out the photo captures from Lily's video. I spend another three hours uploading the files to a cloud account I have set up, and run some scripts to mirror the files elsewhere. At 11 p.m. I go back to the hotel and sleep, setting the alarm on my watch for 1 a.m. but knowing I won't need it.

TWELVE

AT 2 A.M. I GO TO TEN HOUSE AGAIN, SITTING IN THE DODGE AND watching the same procession as the night before from the alley adjacent to the building's north side. Each time the man goes inside, I view the door through my binoculars. When I see it draw in twice against the frame, I know it's locked from the inside.

Five minutes later I open the door with the pry bar on the hinge side, tearing the screws out from the wooden frame and letting the door fall to the pavement. I walk partway into the hallway, holding out the gun I took from the man the previous night. The pile from the ruined video equipment is still there, the rest of the rooms empty as before.

I walk back to the Dodge for my tools and the gas jug, and then back through the same hallway again, past the rooms and the closet and up the stairs. The lights in the main room are on, illuminating the club in all its disrepair and stark ugliness, but I don't see anyone. The music is on lower than before, but I can still feel it in my bones, a slow, methodical beat. I wonder why it's on at all, but I keep moving forward.

I walk through the VIP section again, parting each curtain with the gun in front of me, until I reach the recessed door at the end. There's no lock this time, so I don't need the pry bar. I walk up the stairs slowly, trying not to make any sounds.

When I reach the top the door to the office is open and a light is on. The door to the bathroom on the right is closed, with a little light coming out from underneath. I kick it open and sweep the gun down and to the right, firing three times as I turn toward where I assume the toilet would be.

All three shots miss. The big man jumps up at me, naked, and nearly knocks the gun out of my hand. I take two quick steps back and hold it level at his head, and continue backing out. I motion with the gun for him to walk toward the office.

I recognize him from the video and from the last time I was here. I want to shoot him right there. The office is empty and the safe is gone, just a hole in the wall.

"Where is Rastov?" I say.

When the man doesn't answer, I shoot him in the left shoulder, the impact of the bullet shoving him back and onto a couch against the wall. When he tries to get up I pull the trigger again, hitting him in the opposite shoulder. He falls back onto the couch and stays there, bleeding and hunched forward. The room is hazy with gunpowder.

"Where is Rastov?" I ask again.

The man grimaces. "You know who we are? You're fuckin' dead, man. Fuckin' dead."

"So are you," I say. "Where is Lily?"

"Who the fuck is Lily?"

"Elle," I say.

I hold up the photo of Lily to his face and he laughs. "The wife?" The man laughs harder now, making the blood from his shoulders run faster, soaking his white shirt. "Sweet piece, that one. She loved it. Even left one of her fingernails in my back. Sweet man. Fuckin' sweet. In the ass too, I tell you. Made little Vicky watch, the rat."

I reach into my pocket, take out the phone I took from him the previous night, and toss it onto his lap. "Call Rastov," I say. "Right now."

"Give me back my gun and maybe I'll put in a good word for you."

I swing the gun against his enormous head, feeling the strike in the bones of my forearm. He nearly passes out from the impact, but somehow he holds his head up.

"Call," I say, pointing the gun at the phone.

He presses some numbers on the glass keypad, and, after several seconds, starts talking into the handset.

"Ask him where Lily is," I say.

He struggles to stay upright on the couch. "Guy who took my gun," he says into the phone, "probably the safe, too. He pauses for a moment, listening to the voice on the other end. "Got a hard-on for the cunt, I dunno."

The big man looks up at me and asks if I have the drive and the papers from the safe. I nod. "Says he'll trade," he says into the phone again. "Wants to know who you are."

I take the drive from my coat pocket and hold it up for him to see. "Trade," I say.

He speaks into the phone once more, wincing and holding it a couple of inches from his face. "Who are you?" he asks again.

"Put the phone on speaker mode and set it on the table and I'll tell you." When the phone is on the table, I kneel down in front of it, my nose nearly touching the rectangular screen. I imagine Rastov's sweating face on the other end, his rotting teeth close against the speaker. I imagine Lily somewhere nearby. I hope she can hear me. I hope she's there, listening. I hope she's alive.

I say: "I'm Lily's brother. Leon. I'm coming for her. And then I'm coming for you."

Still kneeling, I swing the gun toward the big man's face and pull the trigger, firing until the gun clicks empty.

I end the call, pocket the phone and walk out of the office backward, down the stairs, around the main floor in a circle and finally out through the basement hallway, pouring

NOISE

splashes of gasoline every few feet. When I reach the outside door, I toss the jug back into the hallway, light a kitchen match and drop it into the puddle. The flames race through the hallway, up the stairs and into the main floor, engulfing Ten House and obliterating the man who touched Lily, and the room where it happened.

I take a photo of the burning building with the man's phone and text it to the last number dialed, and then I throw the phone into the flames and walk back to my truck.

THIRTEEN

"RECOGNIZE THE GIRL?" RICO SHIFTS HIS BODY FORWARD AND points to a photo of Sara spread-eagled on the collapsed roof of a white four-door sedan, blood running down the hood, the sides of both front doors and the collapsed windshield. He'd picked me up at the hotel at around 9 a.m., no warning. Said I wasn't under arrest. His shirt and jacket were rumpled and he smelled like coffee and old beer, like he'd worked through the night.

She's dead? I turn the pad toward him.

"Obviously, genius. She texted your number yesterday, so as of now you're her last known contact."

We met in Brooklyn, I write. *I dropped her at work afterwards.*

"Right," Rico says. "Or you got pissed off, hit her a little too hard? See the way the cheeks are caved in like that, all distorted? Prelim says it was a very big fist, M.D. says look for someone with big hands, swollen knuckles and the like. She was alive when she hit the roof of the car, eight stories south from her bedroom window, hence the blood was still pumping out. Took a bit of time."

I stare at the photo as he watches me.

"Then there's the roughed-up cook, fan of the Lily porn you and Jane shared over coffee, and a break-in and subsequent fire, also—you guessed it—in the very site of the aforementioned Lily porn."

Where's Jane? I write.

"Fuck off is where Jane is. Worry about me. I looked into the address you gave on your missing persons report. It's a construction site for an office park that isn't even built yet. Lie number one, Leon."

I live where I work, I write.

"Yeah, I heard that. Supervisor says you're fired, by the way. You forgot to tell him about your little vacation to the Big Apple. Also, traffic cams show your piece-of-shit truck near the site of two crimes: a break-in and fire at a strip club in Astoria, and a beat-to-death, dropped-on-a-car stripper in Bushwick, Brooklyn."

Where's Jane? I write again.

"Says here you took the Army for a ride through college?" he says, ignoring me. "What do they want with deaf guys? Fuckin' useless."

NOISE

Lip-reading and body cues, I write. *With the right equipment, I can decipher what you're saying from a mile away.*

He pauses at that, staring. "Yeah. And what the fuck is fast-bridging and excavation? That some kind of shorthand for stripper-beating and fire-mongering?"

Where is Jane?

Rico ignores me, rubbing the back of his hand against the stubble on his chin. "Undergrad, honors, major . . . geology? Deaf guy studying rocks? No wonder you live in a truck. And what the fuck is Surma? Dambe? And wait . . . Piper Knife Fighting?"

African martial arts. It's how children survive in a world even a New York City cop couldn't fathom, I think to myself. But I don't say anything.

"Here's what I think. I think you're in a fuckload of trouble here in the Big Apple, Leon. Even if you stay out of jail, which you won't, you'll never leave here alive. These Russians will kill you, believe you me. Those films are just a hobby. I know Jane's got a soft spot for you, got herself a little retard brother, too; wears himself a helmet to dinner and such. But I'm an only child, Leon, so we're all good there."

Rico checks his phone, scrolls through several messages, and then rubs his cheeks again and tries to smooth his hair back in the same awkward movement. Just as he starts talking again Jane walks in, angry and out of breath. She leans into his ear and says something I don't catch and they walk out of the interrogation room.

I look at the photo of Sara, remembering our dinner the previous night. I shouldn't have let her go. She's dead because of me. Guy who killed her, also dead, maybe, but that doesn't matter much to her, or to me. She wasn't in any of the videos. She worked for a veterinarian. She had a kid. She was Lily's friend. She should have gotten away.

Geology is the study of pressure and time. It is what happens to ordinary things when both are applied. Given enough time, a small fissure in the ocean floor becomes a tsunami that wipes out an entire coastline a thousand miles away. Cities fold upside down in massive earthquakes and are swallowed up whole. A volcano becomes a thousand tons of molten rock, obliterating everything in its path.

A river becomes a canyon. A rabbit becomes a diamond. A continent vanishes into the sea and is never seen again. A small boy from Africa becomes a murderer. Nature kills us all.

I want to go back home, but my home was always Lily.

FOURTEEN

JANE COMES BACK INTO THE ROOM ALONE, LOOKING SIMILARLY disheveled and very tired. "The fire," she says, sitting in the chair opposite me. "A man died."

"His hands," I say, still looking at the photo on the table in front of my hands. "He killed Sara."

"What do you want, Leon? You know that's not how this works. You know how it ends."

"Where's Lily?" I say.

Jane looks at me, still angry. "The videos," she says. "We have Rastov and The Bear on assault, rape and battery. We'll get it done the right way."

"Where are they?" I stare at her eyes. She doesn't answer.

"That cop?" I say. "The one who got shot . . . what does he have to do with Lily?"

"He recruited her, he ran her. We've been looking into the Russians for a long time. The club is nothing, the videos . . . nothing. No victims ever came forward. He's into bigger things. We know what, we're just not there yet."

Jane pauses, looks down and then continues, the movement of her lips less pronounced. "We turned the husband, Victor. That's where Lily came in."

"She volunteered?"

Jane says nothing, looking down at the photo of Sara again.

"Before or after the video?" I ask.

"What?"

"The time stamp on the video, nine days ago." I say. "Before or after?"

"Long before," she says.

"So you could have prevented all of this."

"It's not that simple, Leon."

"What did you have on her?"

Jane looks up. "What did you say?"

"You said you turned the husband. Did you use her to get to him, or him to get to her?"

Jane doesn't say anything.

I stand up to my full height, leaning over the table and towering over her. "You compromised Lily," I say, leaning over the table. "Probably a photo with the cop having a fucking coffee with my sister in that diner. You showed that photo to the husband and threatened to expose Lily if he didn't turn. He's legit, afraid of what his family would do to her. Then you leaked the photo to the father to pressure him to act, and they punished Lily to get to Victor and to cut off your leverage. She never knew anything."

"I didn't leak the photo." She lifts her eyes to meet mine.

"Lily would never work with the police."

"You don't know that."

"I know my sister," I say. "She would have stayed out of it. She strung you along to buy herself time. That's why Sara contacted me. That's why the cook had the video. That's why the cop never pulled her out, because she was already out."

"We'll find her, Leon. It's what we do."

"You didn't even know about the video," I say. "People like Lily, like Sara, like the cook, to them you're no different than the Russians. It's them against everyone, and everyone against them."

Jane picks up her papers in short, exaggerated movements and walks around me to the door. "Stay out of it, Leon. Let us do our job."

Pressure and time.

FIFTEEN

THE POLICE RELEASE ME SEVERAL HOURS LATER AND I WALK BACK to the hotel, stopping at a falafel truck on the way, and then spend the rest of the afternoon going through the papers I took from the office. There's not much there, some cryptic spreadsheets and scanned documents with no obvious addresses other than the building itself, but I force myself to reread them all several times before falling asleep at the little desk by my window.

When I awaken, it's already dark. Jane had said the club was nothing, a hobby for Rastov, that they're into bigger things. Then I remember the bouncer from the club, and Jane's comment that he and Rastov go way back. Then I wonder if he worked for the father and was assigned to Rastov instead of the other way around, him working under

Rastov for the club. If the club was used to wash money, then it makes sense to structure it that way. Besides, he was too calm, too composed, to be just muscle.

Then I remember the papers I took from him the night before and I get lucky. What look like pallet numbers, weight and shipping schedules from an address in Gowanus, by the old Brooklyn waterfront.

I take the address to the Internet café and rent time on a Mac. From satellite photos on Google Earth it looks like a small warehouse in a run-down commercial area, obscured by the elevated Route 278, a busy artery looping around the western curve of Brooklyn and heavily traveled by trucks. I Google the street address I found on the shipping manifests but nothing comes up, so I spend the next several hours researching the buildings and history of the area. There had been several gentrification efforts, including abandoned subway extensions that ran into several lines of underground freight tunnels near the old warehouse district. The geography was considered compromised and not suitable for rezoning for any new structures above fifty feet. The tunnels were abandoned. I print out a few of the map pages and then catch the train back to my truck.

I make a single pass of the warehouse in the truck, driving slowly enough to make out structural details but fast enough to look like I'm going somewhere. It's about a quarter-mile from a feeder canal that dumps into the Upper Bay across from New Jersey, close enough to have direct drainage but also far enough to contain stable sub-levels. It's an artificial shore, marsh into backfill atop the underlying glacial granite that forms much of the Northeast. I drive by the other areas I marked on the map where the construction was supposed to have been started and abandoned, where the original freight tunnels supposedly ended. Even if the police know about the warehouse, people and materials could move underground in small volumes and remain undetected, exiting from any of several egress points along the tunnels, or even the drainage pipe toward the bay and into a small bay skiff or a fishing boat.

Or it could be nothing at all.

By 6 a.m. I'm back in the Stardust, and by 9 a.m. I'm standing in line at the Midtown Branch of the New York Public Library. I use my expired university I.D. to gain entry to the older research building on the west side of Fifth Avenue. I tell the receptionist at the main desk that I'm researching public utilities projects in support of gentrification, and the urban flight that results when projects are defunded, blocked, or simply abandoned. She directs me to another room, where an intern is assigned to help me. I don't know whether this is standard procedure or a handicap issue, and I don't really care. The intern is young and blonde, with a rail-thin body and thick, serious glasses that make her head look comically small. She's probably a student herself. But she likes my fake project, and says she's eager to help.

Six hours later, I have more than I could possibly need.

Approved project plans. Construction routes. Elevation maps. Drainage diagrams with capacity planning and metrics. Yard-by-yard summaries in support of the rezoning effort. A plan to shore up the existing freight tunnels to route the extension of the existing subway lines. A final addendum to backfill the tunnels with concrete to circumvent the height restrictions of the rezoning rule, since building fifty-foot-high residential complexes is not economically feasible.

When a project is defunded in New York, or wherever private contractors bid on a project, it ends instantly, the equipment withdrawn and doors padlocked, nailed shut, or covered over.

There is no exit plan. Officially, it just ends.

SIXTEEN

I PARK THE TRUCK IN A STRIP MALL IN FLATBUSH AND FIND another Internet café, this time searching through the commercial rental listings on Craigslist. Several hours and phone calls later I find what I'm looking for and drive back to Brooklyn again, stopping once for gas. I pull the truck into a street-level garage in Red Hook, near the Gowanus Canal, and hand $120 to an old Peshawar woman in a turban. She hands me a key and walks away.

I empty the truck and organize my belongings on a worktable against the side wall of the garage and then curl up in the back of the truck and fall asleep.

From the moment I arrived in South Carolina, Lily began drawing Africa for me, hundreds of drawings of deserts, of sunsets, of people riding elephants to work, of giraffes carrying picnic baskets, of zebras pulling lovers in wagons, of lions, majestic and serene and powerful, overseeing all.

But her Africa is not my Africa. I had a better chance of seeing the Tooth Fairy than I ever did of seeing a lion, and if I ever had seen one I'd have run like hell. But if Lily had seen a lion, she'd have run right up to it. She'd have hugged it and asked it to eat carrots instead of deer or rabbits. And the lion, of course, would have listened.

Americans are dreamers, civilized people, civilized in a simple, beautiful way, in a way the rest of the world just isn't. People in America say you can be whoever you want to be, you can dream, you can choose, you can create your life as you want it to be, but this isn't true in much of the world, and it certainly isn't true in Africa. You are what Africa makes you; you become what she requires of you.

We have the same view of safari as kids in Harlem have of Disneyland. We know it exists, we know it's for other people, we know we'll never see it, and if we did see it, we know we would hate the world that created it and excluded us.

And we know that lions don't eat deer and rabbits because they have no other choice, or because they're hungry, or because they don't know any better, or because they are lazy. Lions eat because they are lions. We fear them most of all, perhaps, for the very fact that they are singular in a way that we could never be, and it is that singularity of purpose that makes them strong.

I sleep poorly. The rumbling outside from the heavy trucks

on 278 overhead disturbs me. I worry about Lily. I wonder where she is, how her life has gone, who she's become. Who I've become. I think about Sara. I think about our mother.

In Lily's world, I am the lion now.

I awaken around midnight and walk back to Gowanus with a flashlight and my duffel bag. It's nearly low tide, so I start at the bay, locating the drainage pipes and mentally diagramming the streets they follow. They pass the warehouse on both sides, and assuming they make no turns or descents, they'd be around twenty feet underneath the basement level of the building.

I walk the streets in concentric circles, spiraling away from the warehouse and noting the geography. If the city attempted to build subways this close to the bay, they'd need to be either astride or below the sewer feeders, with regular access shafts. It would be a massive, expensive project, taking years, and much of the work done below the water line, but even if the project were abandoned, the tunnels would likely be sealed to remain dry.

According to the initial rejections of the rezoning plan, there was a maintenance shaft abutting the street adjacent to the warehouse, paralleling the smaller sewer feeder lines branching up toward the building. If the maintenance shaft dropped directly into the abandoned tunnels, they could lead anywhere. But I could spend a week wandering around down there and find nothing. Or they could be collapsed, filled in, or not even built at all.

Several hours later, I circle back to the waterfront. By 3 a.m. I haven't seen a single person or car, so I break into the warehouse, using the pry bar against a small waist-high window on the side of the building facing the water, where it's darkest.

I drop my bag to the floor inside and then slide in feet first, my shoulders just squeezing through the small window. The drop is around eight feet, and I land hard, losing my footing and falling sideways onto the floor, gashing my chin on the rough cement. I turn over and lie on my back, giving my eyes time to adjust to the darkness and waiting for the dizziness to pass.

After several minutes I push myself to my feet, brushing the dirt from my arms and face, and start walking around the perimeter of the open space. I cross the width of the warehouse several times. I open a couple of wooden shipping containers with the pry bar, but unless Lily is sleeping inside one I really don't care what they're transporting.

The main room is about a hundred yards across, with a catwalk level leading to a glassed-in office suspended in the corner, halfway between the floor and the roof of the building. Under the office is a slanted hatch-style door, most likely the entrance to a basement. The ceiling is strung with industrial barn-style incandescent lights, hanging in midair like spiders.

I walk up the catwalk to the office first, kicking open the locked door and going through every drawer and cabinet but finding nothing that looks interesting. And no safe. After checking the floor and walls for hidden compartments, I go back down the catwalk and head toward the basement hatch beneath the suspended office.

I drop through to the basement level and start searching again, this time using my flashlight to push back the darkness. The ceiling is much lower here, just barely allowing me to stand upright. It's a full-size basement, nearly as large as the building itself, but mainly empty, just some boxes and overhead pipes and electrical lines, not much that looks used at all.

After several minutes of crossing the basement in a grid pattern, the flashlight catches a reflection of something square and shiny in the far corner of the room. I abandon the grid search and walk directly toward the reflection, realizing about halfway there that it's a standup washer/dryer combo, relatively new. I open the doors to both appliances, but find nothing, not even clothes. It's not bolted down, so I slide it over along the wall, revealing another hatch in the floor, this one much smaller than the upper hatch, and unlike the first one, sunken flush into the concrete floor.

I open the hatch, and drop into hell.

SEVENTEEN

THE LOWER LEVEL IS A MUCH SMALLER ROOM, CONSISTING OF A single hand-dug hallway lined with cages: shiny, thin-gauged enclosures lining the sides of dirt floor, about the size that research labs would use to house lab chimpanzees. There are no lights, and the dirt walls and floor absorb much of the beam from the flashlight, sending very little light reflecting back, and no scatter to the sides. The hallway itself is only around nine feet wide, leaving less than two feet of space to walk between the cages.

I shine the light into the first cage on my right. Inside the tiny cage are a filthy woman and three children wedged behind her, pressing their bodies against the back of the cage. As my light reaches the children, they cover their eyes with their hands, screaming and making the entire cage shake and rattle. The smell of excrement and vomit is excruciating, making me retch, and my eyes tear.

I walk to the end of the hallway and open the cages one by one with my pry bar, walking backward and switching sides with each lock I break open. When I reach the beginning of the hallway, where I first entered, I watch as the women and children emerge, quickly huddling at the far end of the hallway, the children clinging onto the women against the dirt wall. They're dressed in American-looking clothes, new and cheap, but filthy. I leave them in the basement and go back up to the main floor to get a cell signal.

I send Jane three consecutive texts to wake her, and when she finally responds I send her the address of the warehouse. Then I rummage through the office and find some cheap food, candy mostly, and some expired crackers. Old and stale, but better than nothing.

When I walk back down the metal stairs to the main warehouse floor, the women and children are already in the room, forming a circle around the work sink and gulping down handfuls of water, the women washing the faces and arms of the children.

I leave the warehouse while they use the sink, returning my duffel bag to the truck and covering it with a blanket, and bring back a box of food I had in the back of the truck. When I return to the warehouse the women and children walk toward me in groups of two or three, forming a semi-circle around me and staring like I'm the first human they've seen in weeks.

Do any of you understand English? I write in my pad and hand the sheet to the little girl closest to me, around seven years old, with dark-blonde curly hair, dressed in clothing at least two sizes too big for her.

"Yes," she says. "I'm from Cleveland."

How long have you been here? I write.

"Are you deaf?" She touches my arm with her fingertips.

Yes, I write. *I cannot hear, but I can understand what you say as long as I can see your face. How long?*

The girl shrugs. "I don't know. At least a month. I was in the mall with my mom and someone grabbed me and put me in the back of a truck with a bunch of other people and we drove all night and have been here ever since."

All of these people were on the truck with you?

"No. Only some." She shakes her head. "Some were here already. The rest went somewhere else a few days later."

I take out the photo of Lily and ask her if she recognizes her. The girl shakes her head no, and passes it around the room without my asking. The photo comes back to me at around the same time Jane shows up.

All of the children are holding hands. No one's seen Lily.

Jane enters the warehouse with at least a dozen uniformed officers. The uniforms immediately go to the children. More people enter the warehouse a few minutes later, including EMT personnel washing faces and hands with a soapy solution and administering first aid where needed, and two additional women handing out water, blankets and protein bars. Jane tells me to go up to the office and wait, staring at me as if she's deciding whether or not to shoot. She sends another officer to stay with me, an older, uniformed cop. He looks tired but kind, with blue eyes and soft gray hair.

EIGHTEEN

TWO HOURS LATER JANE COMES UP TO THE OFFICE AND RELIEVES the man with the gray hair. She sits in an office chair, exhausted.

"Just stumbled across this place?"

"I don't sleep much," I say.

She raises her hands behind her head and tightens her ponytail. Her shirt is filthy and torn, the underarms stained with sweat.

"You're in a lot of trouble, Leon."

"I need to find Lily. I owe her."

"What does that even mean?"

"This place." I change the subject. "Still nothing?"

Jane sighs. "We've known about this place for a while now. Never saw anything. We've been stopping the trucks for traffic citations, cursory searches. Never found anything. Carpets. Toys. Garbage."

"But you couldn't have known which trucks were coming here," I say.

Jane tilts her head, looking up at me. "No, not really," she says. "Not enough manpower. It was pretty much a cold lead until the undercover cop was killed, which turns everything white-hot again. Even the remotest leads get chased down. But since then there's been no activity here at all."

"Yes," I say, apparently loud enough to startle her. "There was activity here, a couple of dozen kids drinking each other's urine to stay alive long enough for you to do something."

She stands and takes a few steps toward me. "You have an anger problem, Leon," she says. "And obvious issues with authority."

"Do you have your radio?"

"Yes, of course." She closes her eyes and tilts her head back toward the ceiling. "Why?"

"See if any of the uniforms have a fire kit in their car."

"A what?"

"Fire kit. Someone will have one," I say. "Just ask."

Five minutes later, another officer enters with a large black canvas bag. Inside are a sledgehammer, a small ax and a pro-bar—a combination ax, crowbar and pick that NYPD often uses—along with some other items I don't need.

"Follow me." I take the bag and stand.

NOISE

She doesn't move, blocking the door with her small body. "It's a crime scene now, Leon. And I'm beginning to think you're just another criminal."

"Your tech team will spend another week analyzing the paint on the walls," I say. "I'm asking for five minutes."

After several long seconds of staring at me she agrees, since I'd already been on the lower level, but she tells me to step where she steps. I direct her back down to the third level, where I found the cages and the people. Portable halogen lights now line the cages, looking like trapped sunflowers sprung from the dirt floors. Every few steps we have to flatten against the wall to allow police carrying bodies to get around us.

They didn't all follow me up. They didn't all survive.

At the end of the hallway Jane stops and lets me squeeze by her, our chests rubbing together in an awkward, almost comical moment. "End of the line," she says.

I nudge her aside from the last cage, identical to the others, the only difference being that this one was unlocked and empty when I arrived. I drag it out of the way along the dirt floor and take her flashlight, shining it on both walls, inch by inch. After a few minutes of studying the walls, I hand her the flashlight and take a step back, nudging her further back into the hallway.

"You stopped the trucks on the way out," I say. "Because it was easier. Because it made sense. Because you didn't have a search warrant. Because you didn't want to tip them off. So you tagged the trucks you knew were coming *from* the warehouse."

"Yes," she says. "What comes in goes out."

"Not here," I say. "Not those people. Not those trucks."

I remove the big sledgehammer from the canvas bag, expecting her to stop me right there, but she doesn't, waiting to see what I do. I don't give her time to change her mind, pushing her further away into the hallway. I swing the giant sledgehammer horizontally in long, slow arcs, facing away from the wall and twisting my body 180 degrees, putting all of my weight into it. Jane starts slapping my back to get me to stop, probably screaming her lungs out, but I keep swinging, ten, fifteen, twenty swings against both walls until the floor is covered in rubble.

When I finish with the wall, I turn back toward her, covered in sweat. She has her gun out, trained on my face. I drop the sledge to the dirt floor and slowly pick up the pro-bar. The air is thick with dust but I can still see the gun. I turn away and insert the long end of the bar into a crack I opened in the corner and start to lever out the wall.

"Locked from the outside," I say, glancing from her face to the gun in her hand. "This is how they left."

Jane lifts her flashlight under her gun hand and holds both outstretched as she walks slowly past me, leaning into the crevice.

"Son of a bitch," she says, reaching for her radio. I clear out the larger bits of concrete from the floor and lever the wall all the way out, revealing a metal ladder affixed to the side wall, going down at least thirty feet into a pitch-black tunnel.

"It opens the other way," I say, "from the outside."

"Son of a bitch," she says again. "How the fuck did you know this was here?"

"Criminals have been digging tunnels since the beginning of crime," I say. "The research library on Fifth Avenue confirmed it. Below this shaft will be another recently dug tunnel leading to the abandoned freight routes used to haul equipment from a planned subway extension that was never finished. Near that somewhere will be a drainage tunnel leading to the Upper Bay. This is how they move the people. This is how they left. This is why there were no people in the trucks."

"Son of a bitch," she says again.

"They knew you didn't have enough for a raid."

She leans backward in a sudden, jerky movement, away from the crevice. "What? How the fuck did they know that?"

"Someone told them," I say. "The break-in at the club changed the equation."

"You sure you weren't a cop in a former life?" She leans forward once again, looking down the shaft and holding on to my arm for balance as she talks into her radio, asking additional units to come down with flares, cameras, more halogens and tech kits. When she finishes, she asks me to follow her back up to the office.

"Is there anything else you're not telling me?" She stares at me, her blue eyes penetrating in the dim light of the single fluorescent tube mounted in the ceiling.

"No." I lean back, slumping against the desk.

"You're sure?"

I keep looking into her eyes but I don't answer.

"We found the cook," she says, looking away from me. "You didn't get the files from him. You got them from the safe."

"I just want to find Lily," I say, my gaze dropping to the floor.

She reaches out with her hand and lifts my chin up. "We have rules, Leon. You broke them."

"I got you the videos and the warehouse."

"Nothing I can use in court."

"Lily isn't in court." I reach into my pocket for my pad, and when I look up Jane has her gun out again.

I write the phone number from the call the bouncer made to Rastov in my pad and hand it to her.

"What's this?" she asks.

"Rastov," I answer.

"Rastov. From the man you shot in the club you set fire to?" She's still pointing her gun at me. "He'll have ditched the phone by now."

"There will be records," I say.

"Again, unlikely anything I can use."

"He raped Lily!" I scream, the sound bringing other officers running up the wooden stairs.

NOISE

"He was a witness," she says, pointing the gun at my face.

"He was a rapist. And he would have gotten out by now. You said it yourself. You have nothing."

"No," she says. "We have the videos. And we have you. Your testimony unlocks the videos. Your testimony gets them into court.

"Leon Palmer," she says. "You're under arrest for the murder of Reynold Taylor, breaking and entering, and arson. And for the murder of Sara Tucker."

"You think I killed Sara?" I say.

"I think you're desperate and dangerous, Leon," she says, keeping her gun aimed at my face in a two-handed stance. "I understand you want to find your sister. But this ends now."

I turn around and put my hands behind my back and she directs another officer to handcuff me.

"I'm sorry, Leon." She looks into my eyes again. "You'll have to leave it to us now."

"So in all of this, I'm the one you arrest?" She stares at me as the second officer handcuffs me and reads me my rights.

"Find Lily," I say, holding her gaze and ignoring everyone else in the room.

"We will."

NINETEEN

RICO PROCESSES ME INTO BOOKING AT THE SAME EAST MIDTOWN station where he took me earlier, and after several hours of intermittent paperwork and waiting, a uniformed officer escorts me into a group cell. There are nearly twenty other men sharing the small space, but no one bothers me, so I sit on a bench and fall asleep.

After what seems like several more hours, another officer wakes me and brings me to an interrogation room, handcuffing me once again to the metal loop bolted to the table. Rico enters a few minutes later, smiling.

"Lily's probably getting gang-raped now, thanks to you," he says, placing a folder on the table and opening it. "I told you not to get involved. I told you to leave it alone. I told you to go home. But you wouldn't listen."

I say nothing, staring at his gray eyes.

"You got us smack-fuck into a federal case now, Leon. If Lily was alive, your actions probably killed her. I told you you'd never leave New York."

I remain still, watching his face oscillate between smugness and fear, erasing whatever lingering doubts I have left.

He picks up my notepad from the table and throws it at my face, the small pad glancing off of my cheek and landing on the floor. "No more little notes, huh, Leon?" His eyes gleam once again. "For a moment I thought you were a little bright, finding those kids, but anyone can shoot a guy and follow an address. And then, of course, go right to prison."

I glance at the notepad on the floor, and look at his face until his smile goes stale. "Can I have a paper and pen?"

He widens his eyes slightly, momentarily taken aback by the sound of my voice. "What the fuck for?" he says. "You're gonna write me a confession? No lawyers like you see on TV?"

"Paper," I say. "And pen."

"OK, Leon." He gets up from the chair. "OK."

He walks around the table and retrieves the pad from the floor, slamming it on the center of the table with enough force that I feel the vibrations down my arms. He leaves the room and returns several minutes later with a pencil stub. "Sorry," he says. "No pens allowed."

NOISE

I take the pencil and start talking as I write slowly, in neat block letters.

"The African lion," I say aloud as I write. "Five of them can take down an elephant. Three a water buffalo. Two a boar. One a deer, if she's patient." I write in neat, even lines. "But you can walk right up to one of them in the wild and they'd just look at you, waiting for you to either leave or attack. There's an unknown tolerance at play, a buffer of observation as perception shifts from offense to defense."

Rico laughs, but as he strains to see the notepad, the laugh doesn't reach his eyes.

"And the males do nothing," I say. "They sit around, yawning. Waiting. Watching. Eating."

"What the fuck does that mean?" Rico's face is once again angry and hot.

"It means you do what you are able to do, what nature and the environment allow you to do and nothing more, so our nature is to construct ways and reasons to do less, until a stronger force pushes us back. It's the basis for physics, for calculus, for crime and society and law. It is the root of everything that governs us. Our downfall is the shortcuts we take to get there."

"Yeah." He snorts. "I have a gun that tells me I can shoot you right now, but a badge that tells me I can't."

"But you want to. You're already imagining scenarios. With me at the center of that fantasy. Because I'm the easiest target. Because I'm the closest. And because I'm the only one you really wanted to catch."

Rico just stares at me, watching the paper in front of me.

"And the only thing a lion truly fears," I say, "is another lion."

I finish writing and turn the pad toward him, sliding it to the edge of the table.

"Last time you brought me in you said traffic cams recorded my truck at a crime scene," I say.

"And?"

"Specifically, you said a break-in and a fire at the strip club."

He realizes what he's reading and looks up at me with pursed lips, his cheeks red and taut.

"But there was no break-in," I say. "Not then, anyway. There was just a fire. You couldn't have known there was a break-in until after the arson investigators determined the origin of the fire and reconstructed the doors and walls in their report, which probably just came in yesterday, or even this morning. The safe was gone before the fire even started. Just a hole in a burnt wall full of holes. In fact, it's very likely that even the arson team would not have discovered the missing safe. But you did."

"What the fuck is this!" He seizes the pad from the table and throws it at my face again.

TWENTY

"RS0211132500. RICO SANTERA. FEBRUARY 11, 2013. $2,500. Payments," I say. "Dates. There's a lot more on the ledger, if you care to see."

Rico stares at me, wide-eyed, as the information sinks in.

"You were told there was a break-in," I say. "Probably right after they discovered it. That's why they abandoned the warehouse. And that's why Jane never found out about it before."

Rico shakes his head, in something of a daze, but says nothing.

"You also said the videos were a hobby," I say. "You're right. No one cares about the videos. Without a corroborating witness it's just snuff. But you couldn't have known I'd gotten the videos from the safe, because you couldn't have known that the safe was even accessed. Unless someone told you."

Rico slowly stands up and faces the two-way mirror, saying nothing that I can see, so I continue. "They wanted the ledger, so they contacted you. Now they want me. So you're going to give me to them. Whether or not you knew about the ledger, that was your plan all along. That's why you wanted to interrogate me alone."

"They'll kill you," he says.

"Probably. Better than rotting in jail for doing what everyone wants to do, but can't." I stare at my hands, cuffed to the small loop welded onto the surface of the table.

"I don't know where Lily is, Leon. And I didn't know about the women and children at the warehouse. I swear it on my wife's grave." He sits back down, all of the former aggression draining from his face, leaving him looking tired and old.

"Listen, Rico," I say. "I don't care what you did or what you know. The world is full of good cops who do bad things, and vice versa. I don't care. I only want to find Lily. So if you don't know where she is, then help me find Rastov and his father."

"So you can kill them? I'm still a cop, Leon."

"If you want to stay a cop, you'll help me."

He says something else but his head is too low for me to see his mouth, so I ask him to repeat.

"I have a daughter," he says. "I can't help you."

NOISE

"There are other names on that list. You'll hurt other cops. Still can't help?"

Rico shakes his head. "Still can't help. I'll take my chances with Internal Affairs. I provide information, just enough to keep them off my back, to keep my family safe. Nothing more. Either way," he says, "you'll go down."

"Three days," I say.

"What? What about three days?"

I say the following words slowly and clearly, knowing that everything else depends upon him believing them, even if no one else would. "In three days the scheduler on my e-mail account releases the ledger, the videos and everything else I found on the hard drive."

"Fuck you!" He jumps back up from the table, facing the mirror again, and then lurches back and grabs my shirt, pulling me halfway across the table until the handcuff ring yanks me to a stop.

"You're a fucking animal, Leon," he says, his mouth inches from my nose. "You really are."

"We do what we are able to do, Rico. We do what we must. How old is your daughter?"

"Nine." He lets go of my shirt and sinks back into the chair across the table from me, his face still angry, but deflating slowly.

"You have a way to contact them?"

"No," he says. "They leave a phone for me in a park nearby, a small chalk mark on a bench indicating contact.

The phone contains a single number. As soon as the job is complete, both numbers get disconnected. Always the same process."

"They raped Lily," I say.

"I can't help you."

"You can."

"I can, but I won't."

"You will," I say. "Someone will get to me in here, and I'll tell them you helped me. They'll want me alive, and you dead."

"I'll do what I have to do to protect my daughter," he says flatly.

"I'll do what I have to do to find Lily."

"Lily's dead," he says.

"You know that?"

"I know them."

"I don't believe you."

Rico sighs, clearly frustrated. "I don't give a rat's fuck what you believe. We're done here." He gets up to leave.

"Wait," I say. He turns around and pauses. "If I find them first, your problems go away, regardless of what happens to me."

"You don't get it, Leon. There are dozens of warehouses like the one you found. And other cops besides me."

"But they'll contact you to make arrangements for me."

"They already know where you are," he says. "They don't need me."

NOISE

"True, but they don't know about the ledger, that it will come out."

"So? They get rid of you, lose a few cops and go on with their business. They don't need me. Or you."

"Shipping manifests," I say. "It wasn't just payments to cops."

"Doesn't mean shit. They'll already have changed all that. Cleared out of the warehouses or whatever. It's over, Leon."

"It's over when I find Lily."

"You're fucking crazy, Leon. It's not worth it. Lily's already dead."

"You don't know that."

"So?"

"So," I say. "You give me to them."

"They'll just kill you."

"Problem solved then," I say.

"Not for me."

"Yes, for you. And for your nine-year-old daughter."

"I don't think so, Leon. I think I'm better off with you right where you are."

"No, Rico," I say. "If I talk to anyone else here about the ledger and the hard drive, I immediately go into isolation as a material witness, and when that happens, all they have left is you."

"And?"

"You're forced to kill me here, in a cell. If you get away with it, your daughter winds up in a video, in a cage, and then you'll do whatever they ask. If you're right about Lily, then you know what they'll do to you. To your family."

"I can't just sign you out."

"You can follow up on a lead. I'm handicapped. I don't remember addresses well, only landmarks. We go for a drive, your chance to close a case."

"It doesn't work like that, Leon."

"This time, it does. If I stay in here you're finished. You know I'm right. Best case you wind up in prison, and you know what they do to cops in prison. I'm guessing there's another phone waiting for you as we speak."

"You're a fucking deaf garbageman living in a truck. How did you even get this far?"

"Back home, when I was seven I could outshoot you. When I was nine I was a competitive street boxer, fighting tourists for naira. By the time I left Africa, still just a child, I'd killed more people than many cops have ever arrested. We do what we can," I say. "What we are able to do. All I want to do is find Lily and go home. I have no interest in a crime family, or with what happens to you. The Bear is a branch in a very large tree. When I get what I want, I stop climbing."

Rico slumps further back into his chair. "Phone came last night, concerning your imminent arrest."

"And?"

"Nothing, yet."

"Make the contact," I say, staring at his eyes, trying to will some energy into him. "Tell them I have the ledger. Within your reach, but not physically here."

"And your little time bomb?"

"You get the kill switch. All I want is Lily."

"How?"

"We stop at an Apple store, let me use a computer. They're paranoid about security. Wash the logs nightly."

"Seriously?"

"All I want is Lily."

"And if she's already dead?"

"Then she's already dead. I go to prison and you wipe the files and take a little heat from Internal Affairs, use me as a witness and cut a deal. I keep everything else to myself. You go on, doing whatever it is that you do, no one the wiser."

"You'd do that?"

"If Lily's dead, I don't have anything else."

He stares at me for a minute longer, and then stands and walks out of the room.

TWENTY-ONE

RICO SIGNS ME OUT OF THE STATION AND WE DRIVE THROUGH THE underground garage in an unmarked gray sedan. The traffic is thick heading out of Manhattan, but with Rico expertly navigating the side streets, and the generous use of his siren, we reach my truck in Brooklyn in around forty minutes. He stops the car in front of the garage and gets out, opening the back door for me, and we walk into the garage together.

"It's not going to work, Leon," he says about the makeshift plan we devised on the ride over.

"You give them the drive," I say, closing the garage door and lighting my camping lantern. "Say I'll trade access to the online account for Lily. You want to get in front of this. They want me. Simple as that." I pull out clothes from the back of the truck that are slightly cleaner than the ones I have on. "That's the only part that has to work for you."

"No," he says. "Give me the drive, wipe the ledger and get in your truck and go."

"You'll kill me." I pull on brown cargo pants, a black T-shirt and a utility vest lined with pockets.

"I know what you think of me. I'm not a killer."

"Anyone who has a nine-year-old daughter is a killer." We lock eyes, neither of us moving for nearly a minute.

Rico breaks first. "You were in over your head the moment you arrived in New York. I'm giving you a chance, Leon. Get lost, and keep the online copies as insurance. Besides, I can't kill you if I don't trust you."

"That makes a lot of sense," I say, repacking my duffel bag.

"You'll always have a copy of the ledger somewhere. I know that. They know that. And you know that."

"No," I say.

"Then take me out," he says.

"Now?"

"No, asshole," he says. "After I send the message. They know I have you. I give them the drive, you have the ledger, you take me out on the way back to them, dump me unconscious on the way somewhere. You'd love to hit me."

"I don't need you to find them, Rico. I only needed you to get me out."

I finish packing the bag and stow it in the front of the

truck. Rico walks stiffly back to his car. I can tell he's scared now. He's right, too. They'll kill him as soon as they get me.

"Send the message, Rico," I say, just as he slams the door shut.

I drive to an Apple store in a small neighborhood mall outside of Forest Hills, Queens, with Rico a few cars behind me. I pull the truck around to the back and park it in the loading bay, the place where customers are sent to pick up items too bulky to walk through the interior corridors, and then I get back in Rico's car and we drive around to the front entrance of the mall.

On the way to the store, Rico confirmed the meeting on his cell phone and texted me the address. He'd wanted me to use his phone to set up the e-mail scheduler for him instead of risking being seen at the Apple store, of course, but I didn't trust his phone, and the truth is that I do want him to get the ledger. I don't know how he initially got mixed up in this, maybe he's a bad cop, but I believe him when he says he doesn't know about Lily. They're just using him, and no matter what, he's useless to them now. Even if they believe him, which they probably don't, he's burned. Either way, I don't care.

We walk into the mall together, him turning to the right and waiting in a bookstore across the aisle from the Apple store, and me turning left, walking past a single guard and through the glass doors. A tall skinny boy with glasses and pimples, probably not even nineteen, greets me a few steps into the store. I point to my ears and shrug, so he knows I'm deaf, and then I point to the table where the MacBook Pros are. He nods, and I walk toward the laptops, slinging the handles of the duffel bag across my shoulder as I make my way deeper into the store. The Pros are more expensive, kept toward the back.

I reach the display table and stop in front of an outgoing model on sale, the one with a traditional spinning hard drive instead of the new solid-state drives. Leaning over the machine, I open the browser and install an add-on called Boomerang, and then I log into an anonymizer site and set up a scheduled e-mail to send a copy of the ledger to Rico's personal e-mail account two days from now. Then I send a regular e-mail to Jane's police account, giving her the address Rico gave me, an IP address of one of the mirror sites housing most of the files, minus the ledger, that she can access immediately. I also send her a short summary of what's happened since my arrest. Rico is her problem now.

I close the laptop and look around the store. To my left is a young girl with huge brown curly hair engulfing oversized headphones. She's oblivious to everything around her as she scrolls through Facebook on another display model. On my right is an older man. I can't see what he's doing, but his face is inches from the screen.

I look around the room once more. The portly security

guard is at the far door, watching the front entrance to the store. The dozens of cameras installed throughout the room mean that security is lax, the common thinking being that most criminals don't want to get caught. Rico is across the hall in the bookstore, glaring at me and looking very much out of place.

I drop my right hand and slowly remove the small sledgehammer from the deep side pocket of my cargo pants, dangling it against my leg, and swing the handles of the duffel bag across both of my shoulders, turning it into a loose backpack. Turning back to the table, I lift the hammer and swing it against the laptop as fast and as hard as I can. After ten swings, the laptop is in pieces, the hard drive ruined. The girl next to me drops her purse and runs. The old man just stares. An alarm goes off somewhere, activating small, flashing blue lights throughout the store. The guard from the front walks toward me as fast as his soft body allows.

I turn and run toward the back counter, knocking over several employees and customers, and hold the sledgehammer in front of me like a ram as I run into the door to the employee/tech section of the store. The door leads into a short, empty hallway, and within seconds, I'm back in my truck, speeding down Queens Boulevard and onto the main highway, Route 495.

Several minutes later Rico catches up to me and we stop behind a furniture store, squeezing both my truck and his sedan between two large cargo trailers.

TWENTY-TWO

THERE ARE FEW CLOUDS IN THE SKY, AND BOTH OF OUR VEHICLES are masked by the dark shadows cast by the trailers. Rico steps out of his sedan, looking around for a half a minute, and then walks up to my truck. "You killed an Apple," he says. "In some circles that's a religious crime."

"Not my first offense," I say, handing him the silver and orange hard drive from the compartment in the center console of the truck.

Rico takes the drive. "This won't work," he says. "They can just take the drive and shoot me."

"Possible," I say, glancing at the rearview mirror, "but not very likely. If you drove right up with me they'd be instantly suspicious. They'd know that you'd know that they'd just shoot us both right then and there. No." I shake my head and write the IP address of one of the mirror sites I set up for the online files, and hand it to him. I lied about the time-bomb thing, of course, but the files are there.

Unlike the other mirrors, and the one I sent to Jane, this site contains only a single PDF file of a shipping manifest, one they'd already have changed. But the contents of the files are not as important as the files themselves. Basic criminals have yet to fully understand that an electronic copy of a piece of paper is vastly different from the original itself. Every file sent over the Internet has a digital footprint, a loose trail of how and where it was accessed, modified, archived and so on. In the digital world of the Internet, files are living, breathing, moving things, and they always leave a trail, and often full archived copies of themselves. If you know how and where to look.

"I'm guessing that they've already threatened your daughter, and probably in person," I say, "so they'd expect you to create some leverage, to withhold something to protect yourself, just like they'd expect me to use the ledger and other files to try to get to Lily."

"So?"

"So they know you'd give up whatever you had under pressure, but they'll also be more willing to go along with you, since you're thinking like they are. There's no reason to shoot you now, when they can shoot you later."

"Comforting," he says.

I start the truck and put it into first gear. "Remember,

line of sight. No more than fifty feet inside the gate, and no turns. Stop the car, shut off the engine, get out and stand next to the opened door with the drive held in front of you. If no one comes within five minutes, you get back in your car and leave."

"OK."

"OK," I say. I let up on the clutch and the truck rolls to a start, just barely squeezing between the parked trailers and onto a service road. We drive through dense traffic for about twenty minutes before turning off the main boulevard and entering an industrial area of Jamaica, Queens. The address they'd given Rico is a rubbish removal and reclamation center, the modern name for a junkyard. A simple fenced property at the end of a run-down street in a rundown neighborhood. The place has an abandoned, nonfunctioning feel to it, matching much of the surrounding area. I slow the truck down at the top of the narrow road as Rico drives further on toward the property.

After finding a suitable vantage point, I turn the truck around and park facing in the opposite direction, shutting the engine and crawling into the back cargo area. Seconds later I'm prone on the floor, resting the barrel of an old hunting rifle on the window jamb of the tailgate, raising and retracting the manual bolt and chambering one of ten 30.06 long rounds. I haven't shot it in years, and I don't expect to now, but the scope is better than my binoculars.

I watch through the scope as Rico drives his sedan down

the slight incline and through the open gate of the barbed-wire fence surrounding the junkyard. After driving a few yards onto the property he turns slightly to the left and stops, a cloud of dust from the gravel driveway briefly encircling his car.

For a few long moments, nothing happens. The dust cloud surrounding the sedan dissipates. Rico opens the driver's door, but doesn't get out immediately. I scan the property with the powerful scope of the old rifle, executing a quick, if rough, grid search. If anyone's there, I can't see them.

The instant Rico steps out of the car I realize I'm wrong. His body jerks backward, slamming into the opened frame of the door. He briefly regains his footing, staggering a few feet away from the car, dropping the hard drive and clutching his waist with both hands. Through the scope on the Winchester, I see the blood spreading through his white shirt. I swing the scope back to the buildings, sweeping for the most probable sniper positions. After another minute or so, I see a flash in a second-floor window. I shift the scope back to Rico; he's clutching his leg now, and then I pivot back to the window. I can see the shooter's head and shoulder hunched against the window frame, not trying to hide now that he's taken the shot. I steady the barrel of the rifle on the tailgate as I exhale, slowly pulling the trigger near the end of my breath. The shooter's head disappears in a puff of red mist.

I slide the bolt back, ejecting the empty shell, and chamber a fresh cartridge from the ten-round clip. I grid-search everything I can see with the scope, window to window to door, down each sightline and back to Rico, but I can't find anyone else, so I widen the grid outward until I spot a slight cloud of dust toward the back of the property, about thirty yards from where Rico was shot and behind two low buildings.

I drop the rifle on the floor of the truck and scramble back into the driver's seat, the engine still warm and starting instantly. I step halfway down on the gas pedal and drop the clutch, spinning the truck around in a blue cloud of tire smoke and rocketing down the hill toward Rico's car.

I pass his sedan on the opposite side at around fifty miles an hour, ripping off one of the mirrors in a flurry of sparks as the heavy truck bounces on the narrow dirt trail separating the two buildings. As I reach the end of the shorter building, I downshift and power-slide to the right, toward where I saw the dust through the scope.

I hit the small BMW sedan in the rear quarter at nearly sixty miles an hour, collapsing the rear half of the car and exploding all six windows. My truck lurches onto its two right wheels, nearly flipping onto its side, before it bounces down hard on the big tires as I let go of the steering wheel and hit the brakes and slide to a halt around thirty feet past the BMW. I rummage on the floor for the rifle, and then exit the truck and look through the scope at the wrecked car.

The BMW is upright with no guns pointing out, so I walk

toward it, sighting the rifle manually over the top of the scope. Fluids leak from beneath the car, but I don't smell fuel as I approach closer and lower the rifle, holding it with one hand by my side.

The occupants in the back seat are obviously dead, their bodies crushed by the collapsed door frames. The driver seems fine, unconscious and trapped by the airbags. Rastov is unconscious in the passenger seat, blood pouring from a gash in his head, and his arm twisted in such a way that suggests a dislocated if not broken shoulder. I jump onto the hood of the car and pull him out through the shattered windshield by his jacket and drag him back to the truck. I throw him in the cargo area behind the front seats and use plastic cable ties to secure his hands and feet and hogtie him, and roll him onto his side.

I get back in the driver's seat, put the truck in gear and turn around. I roll back over the dirt road toward where Rico lies next to his sedan. The truck is only slightly damaged, the solid steel frame taking most of the energy from the hit and transferring it to my shoulders, which feel like they've been shot even though I braced for the impact.

Rico is still cursing and clutching his nine-millimeter service pistol as I approach. I leave the truck running and exit, picking him up as gently as I can, pocketing his gun as I do. I carry him back to the truck and lay him on the floor next to the unconscious Rastov. Back behind the wheel, I watch

NOISE

Rico's mouth in the rearview mirror as he curses constantly. Even backward, I catch most of it.

The nearest hospital is Jamaica Medical Center, ten minutes away. I stop in the ambulance bay and pull Rico out carefully. Carrying him into the trauma ward, I yell that an officer has been shot.

Several hospital workers spring into action, surrounding me and removing Rico from my arms. Within seconds, he's on a gurney rolling toward surgery and I'm running back to the truck, knocking over doctors, nurses, guards and anything else in my path. After less than two minutes in the hospital, Rastov and I speed away in the truck with four security guards running after us, screaming and inexplicably waving their walkie-talkies.

TWENTY-THREE

I DECIDE TO DRIVE NORTH FOR A WHILE, INSTEAD OF GOING BACK to the garage, to get away from the city. I don't know why, exactly; I don't even know that it's a conscious plan. But I drive across the George Washington Bridge into New Jersey, and then north up the curvy, scenic Palisades Parkway, finally onto Interstate 87 through upstate New York. The sky is slate-gray and large snowflakes land and melt on the windshield of the Dodge.

The drive itself is beautiful. It's difficult to imagine that there exists an entirely different world less that twenty miles from one of the largest cities on Earth, but there it is, and I find myself slowing just to take it all in.

Three hours later, I stop for gas and check on Rastov in the back. He's conscious, but he doesn't look so good, so I fill the tank and start searching side roads. We drive through the thickening snow into the mountains of New Paltz, a college town far too crowded for me, and then toward Kingston, finally west toward Binghamton, staying on small side roads and farm trails.

The roads get progressively worse as I drive north and west, the big tires of the truck crunching through snowdrifts and bits of trees knocked down from the storm. The layer of snow on the ground makes the drive feel softer, grander and more peaceful than it really is.

Halfway through the fresh tank of gas, Rastov pops his head up above the back seat. He's talking, but since I can't read lips so well backward, I ignore him, focusing instead on the increasingly narrow and overgrown roads.

Several hours later, after at least a dozen dead ends and another refill of the tank, I find a small cabin with no tracks on the driveway or the two small roads leading up to it. I pull the Dodge behind it, crushing through several bushes and small trees before coming to a halt beside the rear door.

I sit in the truck for an additional ten minutes, leaving the engine running, the clutch against the floor and the transmission in first gear, until I'm confident that the cabin is empty.

I walk to the back of the truck, pushing Rastov away from my toolbox and grabbing a screwdriver from the top tray. I'd spent much of the drive up amusing myself by calculating the odds on whether he'd be able to free himself from the cable ties, but he hadn't even tried, even with the tools just inches from his hands.

I close the toolbox and take it, along with my bag from the front seat, and open the rear door of the cabin with the screwdriver. The interior of the cabin is sparse and functional... and very cold. A single wooden bed in the corner, a desk, couch, small work/dining table with one chair and a cast-iron wood-burning stove in the center of the room. I get the stove going with lighter fluid and quarter-cut logs from a stack near the front door, leaving an iron fireplace poker wedged between the burning logs, and then I walk back outside to the truck, yanking Rastov through the tailgate window and carrying him into the cabin. His body is so thin that I worry I'll break him, but I drop him on the floor anyway.

I cut the plastic ties securing his hands to his legs with my knife and then pull him upright into the one chair in the room, using additional ties on his forearms and shins to secure him to the chair. Staring at me like a trapped animal, he puts up no resistance.

I go back to the truck and return with my coffee pot and mug, filling the pot with water and coarse grounds and putting it on top of the wood stove. Several minutes later I strain the strong, thick coffee into the mug, blowing on the surface and sipping slowly. Rastov stares at me through two more cups, before finally breaking the silence.

"You shot Reynold," he says.

"Tell me where Lily is." I stand near the wood stove, rubbing my hands to warm them.

"No," he says, without emotion. The heat does little to revive him.

"Why not?" I pick up a short, wood-handled spade shovel leaning upright against the cabin wall and approach him. "It would be better for you if I found her. Then I would leave."

Rastov laughs for nearly a minute, spit leaking down his chin, and then stops. "Lily's a whore. We did little Vicky a favor." He stares at the shovel and squirms against the back of the chair.

I swing the shovel up and rest it on my shoulder.

"Yeah, motherfucker," he says. "The easy way or the hard way? Like a fucking movie. You'll never make it anyway." He strains against the plastic ties. "You're too fucking stupid. So was your bitch."

"No, Rastov." I swing the shovel against his face, the impact snapping his head sideways. "There's no easy way. Not for any of you. Not any longer. You're going to tell me where she is."

"She's dead, asshole," he says, blood pouring steadily from his face onto his lap. I'd hit him a little too hard with the shovel.

"Then there's a body somewhere. Let me bury her. Think, Rastov."

"I don't know nothing." He spits out more blood. "I just do the club."

NOISE

"I don't believe you," I say. "Convince me."

I remove the iron fireplace poker from the stove and touch it to the left side of his neck, an exquisitely sensitive area of skin, and hold it there for several seconds. The smell of melting flesh is excruciating. I can only imagine how he feels, but I force myself to smile. He howls and shakes, knocking himself over and trying to push himself along the floor with his chin, which doesn't work at all.

"I don't know where she went, I swear," he says as I yank him back upright. "I don't know anything. I just do the club." He's crying openly now, like a small, frail child. "Reynold don't even work for me, he worked for my father. No one trusted me. Said I was too unstable. Like the pipe too much."

At least I was right about that. "After that night, after you raped her, you never saw her again?"

"No. I'm telling you, she just ran. No one's seen her since. I swear it. I'd tell you, man," he says, sobbing. "I know you're doin' right, family and all. I'd do the same, I would. And I didn't rape her, neither. Wouldn't have been able to, physically and all."

Without thinking, I raise the shovel, desperately wanting to hit him again, harder, but I catch myself just in time. "Tell me where your father is."

"What? No way. Now you're fucking crazy. Even if I did, you'd never get at him. He's been doing this for a hundred years. He's smart, and sly as a fox."

I can barely understand him now, his face distorted too

much from the swelling. "Then there's no reason not to tell me, is there?" I pull back his middle finger slowly until it snaps.

"Fuck you! Fuck you! Fuck you!" The chair jumps and bucks with each word. He screams unintelligibly for several minutes. The fire heats the small place, making the area seem smaller, the air itself oppressing to my senses.

"California? Las Vegas? Harlem? Tell me, Rastov," I say, leaning toward his head and yelling in his ear. "Tell me and you can walk home, take your chances in the cold. Maybe you warn your father, he comes to get you, sees how you saved him, sees how important you are to the family."

"You'd do that?"

"If he knows where my sister is, then I have to speak with him. It's important to me that I find her," I say.

"I can't."

"Yes, Rastov, you can." I break another finger.

I wait until he finishes screaming, which goes on for several minutes longer, and then I grab his greasy hair with my right hand and yank his head back, just short of breaking his neck.

"OK OK OK OK!" he says. "Meatpacking."

"Give me a fucking address!" I pick up the chair with him in it and throw both across the room and onto the worktable against the far wall, shattering both the table and Rastov's chair.

I walk back toward him as he crawls along the planked, wooden floor, bits of the chair still secured to his limbs with the plastic ties. "Last chance," I say, dragging him upright by the neck and holding him against the wall with my left hand, his feet dangling a foot in the air.

After a few seconds, he gives me an address near the end of Fourteenth Street, on Manhattan's West Side.

I look at him for a moment longer, feeling sorry for him. Then I remember Lily, walking toward the camera at the end, defiant and broken.

"I believe you, Rastov." I lean away from him and then swing my weight back toward him, driving my right fist into his head and crushing his gaunt face. His body goes limp, and I drop him onto the floor.

I look around the cabin for anything that might be useful but find nothing, so I grab the shovel and Rastov and walk out of the cabin and into the woods.

I don't want to leave his body where it might scare someone, found by little kids playing in the snow, but the ground is far too frozen for the shovel, so I drop Rastov into a ditch deep in the woods and walk back toward the cabin.

I douse the fire and gather the pieces of the table and chair into a corner, admiring the cabin and feeling a sudden, intense loneliness. I could live here, I think to myself. I really could.

Several minutes later I drive the truck a few miles up the dirt road, turn off into the woods and crawl in the back to sleep.

It is very late.

TWENTY-FOUR

I AWAKEN BEFORE DAWN WITH THE TRUCK BURIED IN A FOOT OF snow and the interior nearly pitch black. I crawl into the front seat and turn the key, pumping the gas several times before the cold engine catches. Once I drop the transmission into first gear and ease out the clutch, the truck instantly breaks free, lurching several feet farther into a cluster of small trees. I leave the truck running and get out, wiping snow from the windows with my hands and making sure the exhaust is clear.

I leave the engine running for a few minutes to warm it while I make coffee in the back of the truck, using my Sterno stove and more of the coarse grounds. The truck is a mess, my belongings scattered around the small cargo area in back, much of them covered in Rastov's blood. I spend a few minutes ordering the clothes and food and tools, make a second cup of the strong, sludgy coffee, and then I get my phone and shut off the engine.

How's Rico? I text to Jane.

She answers instantly: *Looks OK, medically induced coma for the trauma. You saved his life. Where are you?*

She doesn't know about Rastov yet. *Far,* I write.

I got your email, she answers.

I sip my coffee slowly, staring at the small screen.

Storm coming, she writes after several minutes.

Literally or figuratively?

Both.

BOLO on me yet? I wonder how hard they'll be looking for me now. Technically, I'm an escapee.

On you? No. Not yet, anyway. Officially, you're still signed out, at least until we hear from Rico or get him overruled. The city will declare a snow emergency at around 6 p.m., slows everything down. It's already getting messy. Sanitation won't plow until the worst passes. Their idea is to let the city shut down, wait it out and save a little cash in the process.

Not a bad idea, I write. *Did you find the shooter?*

Most of him, she answers. *Who was in the passenger seat? Rastov?*

Are you tracing my cell? I ask.

I'm still reviewing the files you sent. It's a mess for a lot of cops. It will take me a little more time to determine the best course of action.

NOISE

Not my mess.

Is that everything that was in the safe, she writes, *or is there more?*

I finish my coffee before responding. *Lily once told me that she imagined she was deaf whenever it snowed. Said the snow blocked out all the ugly things. She was right. It's beautiful, up here. Not like the South. Not like back home.*

The snow or being deaf?

I stow my portable stove and coffee cup. A moment later, I'm turning the truck around and rolling back out the way I came.

My phone buzzes in the center console. On the screen is a one-word message from Jane. *Leon?*

More, I write, answering her earlier question. *More than you'd want to see.*

I stay on the side roads, relying on my compass to keep me heading roughly toward the city. The truck is steady up to around forty miles an hour in the fresh snow, a bit faster where it's packed down by other vehicles, but visibility continues to deteriorate. I believe Jane when she says they're not looking too hard for me, but the New York State Thruway would be plowed and salted, and whatever police were on shift would use it anytime they had to go north or south. A big gray truck with South Carolina plates doesn't exactly blend in.

I stop in Newburg for food and some supplies. At the local Home Depot I pick up some fertilizer, a can of powdered aluminum used in portable welding rigs, another gas can, some quarter-inch rope, and a box of safety matches. A few towns further south I find a Target, picking up a couple of Styrofoam coolers, a dozen empty Mason jars with screw-on metal caps and a large metal pot used for planting trees.

Just like that, the last of my cash is gone.

Part of me knows what I am getting into. The rest doesn't care.

Three hours later Jane texts again, three words this time: *Be careful, Leon.* I stop once to siphon fuel out of a mobile home. Four hours after that I'm back at the garage in Red Hook.

TWENTY-FIVE

I SHUT THE DOOR TO THE GARAGE WITH THE TRUCK INSIDE AND unload the bags from the back, lighting my lantern and placing it on the worktable against the wall. I crush the Styrofoam coolers into crumbs with my hands, dropping enough of the pieces into the metal planter to form a layer about an inch deep, then add the fertilizer and the silver welding powder, and then mix in the gasoline as the Styrofoam dissolves into a thick, gray liquid.

I punch holes in the aluminum covers of the Mason jars, stopping periodically to stir the contents of the planter and add more gasoline, Styrofoam and the aluminum and fertilizer. As the mixture continues to thicken, I thread a foot of rope through each of the covers, folding the rope sideways against the metal and securing the tops with duct tape.

Finally, I pour in the thick liquid and screw the covers back on the jars, with the ropes looping through the tops.

By the time I start packing up the truck it's nearly 3 a.m. I take everything with me.

The only person who can, or will, tell me what happened to Lily is her husband. I know where to find him; he brags about his apartment in Tribeca on his Facebook account. But from the moment I saw the video, the first time I'd seen my sister in ten years, right then I knew what I would do.

I know who I am. And who I was, back in Africa. We were never meant to get old. Certainly never meant to come here, to a country of laws and institutionalized cruelty and slow, stretched-out death. I think Lily knew what would happen when she contacted me. She knew I would see the video. She knew what it would do to me. She knew what I would do to the people who made it. And she knew she'd never see me again. Or want to.

Anyone who says that people cannot change has never survived a rape.

Bad people get worse. Good people just hide. Lily was wrong about me. I'm not a lion. Rico was right. I'm a deaf garbageman living in a truck, waiting to die. I could have gone to Victor first. I could have let Jane do her job. I could have been a better brother. I could have done anything.

But all along, I've just followed the trail of crumbs she left for me. When there are no people in your life, all that remains is to follow ghosts.

TWENTY-SIX

I BACK THE TRUCK OUT OF THE GARAGE AND INTO A FULL-SCALE blizzard, the thick snow blowing horizontally and piling up against everything in its path. Though I slept for several hours, I don't feel rested at all.

I make it all the way to the Manhattan Bridge without seeing any other vehicle. The fuel gauge reads just slightly above empty. As I drive across the East River, I can see that the bottom half of Manhattan is dark. There are no overhead lines in Manhattan to be pulled down by trees or ice, and it's an unusually large area for a routine outage, so most likely it's a blown transformer, not from the snow but from flooding. The blizzard struck land during the full moon at an incoming tide. Tomorrow they'll call it a freak event, a "once-in-a-century storm" that hits every few years. Sara would have blamed it all on my truck, had she lived to see it.

I coast down the lower roadway of the Manhattan Bridge, leaving the truck in neutral and feathering the brakes, and then onto Bowery, engaging the transmission and turning off at Hester Street. I take side streets the rest of the way, heading north and west through Chinatown, Little Italy, Soho and Tribeca, turning up Greenwich Avenue around twenty minutes later. Jane was right. No snowplows. No cars, and, with this much wind, not even pedestrians.

Visibility is little more than ten feet as I drive up Fourteenth Street in the pitch-black night. The snow is at least a foot and a half deep, but the truck holds steady. I turn at Ninth Avenue and drive south for a few blocks, and then loop back around to Tenth Street and head north, rolling past the address Rastov gave me at the cabin.

The building is an old three-story brick building, with a garage and loading bay on the first floor, one of the few remaining beef companies in an area once dominated by slaughterhouses. The second floor could be an apartment, or more likely an office for the business downstairs. It's impossible to tell in the dark. The third floor, however, has curtains.

I park the truck in an alley adjacent to the building. Covered in snow, the Dodge can easily pass for a commercial vehicle, and even if there were patrols looking for me, it would be covered soon enough. I get my bag from the cargo area, along with two of the Mason jars and the gun I

NOISE

took from Rico, and make my way back to the short brick building.

There are old vent-style windows on the first floor, and vertical sliders on the second and third. I walk around the back of the building, the wind and snow cutting visibility down to near zero now. It's a little better in the alley, but I still have to hug the wall and lean forward against the wind.

After walking along the length of the wall, my hand hits an iron drainpipe coming from the roof. I could climb it, but then I have no idea what's on the roof, or how sturdy the rusted supports fastening the drainpipe are, or whether I can even make it to the top at all, so I circle the building again.

The residential entrance is a single door a few feet north of the loading bay, an imposing, fortified steel door with a round buzzer in the center and an encased metal frame to discourage pry bars. I might be able to get at it with the sledgehammer, but it would take too much time, and would be very loud. Same problem with the lower windows; the glass in each small panel contains shatterproof wire mesh. I'm not sure the noise would even matter out here, muffled by the snow, but I decide to keep looking.

Twenty minutes later, I am back in the alley climbing up the four-inch drainpipe, terrified of losing my grip on the icy pipe and falling to the street. The handles of my duffel bag are wrapped around my ankle and dragging against the wall beneath me as I ascend. I creep up slowly like an inchworm, contracting and stretching, inch by inch, the bag dragging two feet below. My hands go numb halfway up, but I keep climbing. I pass two windows, dark and out of reach, before levering myself over the ledge and rolling into the deep snow on the roof. I lay there for several minutes, my eyes staring up at the swirling snow, my chest heaving for air.

I catch my breath and start to rise, but the wind is much stronger up here, forcing me to crouch and walk slowly. Eight or nine yards away there's another steel door set into a wall beneath a gravity-fed water tower; a huge, metal cylinder around forty feet high, perched atop a wooden structure that looks like something out of a farm back home.

I creep up to the door, spreading my weight as evenly as possible and approaching with the pry bar. The door is flush-set and fortified like the one in the first-floor entrance. I don't see any other access point on the roof, nor is there a fire escape leading back down from the third-floor windows, which seems odd in New York City.

I press the light on my LED watch. It is just after 4 a.m. Shielding the beam with my hands, I shine my flashlight on the base of the tower. It's a standard 4x4 support structure, with four newer-looking 2x4 planks wedged diagonally between the surface of the roof and the curved wall of the water cylinder itself for additional support.

I loosen the base of one of the diagonal support beams with the pry bar, detaching it from the roof and walking sideways with it until the other end breaks free from where it's attached to the cylinder itself, maybe eight feet up. The support drops to the surface of the roof, disappearing in a puff of snow. I repeat the process for the remaining three supporting planks, trying to make as little noise as possible.

Even with the gale-force winds, the tower does not move. The additional supports were probably just added in response to a code violation. I walk around the entire tower again, pushing my weight against the four remaining vertical beams holding the massive tower, but the structure doesn't budge.

I return to the south side of the tower where I first started, locating my duffel bag, already covered in fresh snow. I remove the long fire ax and walk back to the first support, which faces the center of the roof. I swing the ax against the interior side of the wooden beam so it buckles away from the tower, arranging my body under the center so I can quickly back away as it falls forward. The original wood is old and soft. After four long, slow swings, the bottom half of the 4x4 falls away, leaving the top half of the beam hanging in midair.

The tower still doesn't move. I look up at the water cylinder, high up in the blizzard on three legs like a mythical, defiant creature, the top barely even visible in the swirling snow. I have an irrational urge to climb the thing, to climb to the top, and keep climbing into the snow.

I walk around to the rear side again and lean against the

base structure of the tower once again, pushing up and against the corner of the lower horizontal braces, and I can feel it give slightly. I pull back on the structure and push again, rocking the tower on its three remaining wooden supports, the wind helping it forward. Push, pull, push, pull. The tower swings back and forth, at least three feet each way, before the second supporting beam in the front buckles and the tower lurches forward.

The metal cylinder crashes onto the center of the roof and through it, collapsing a large section of the roof and the floors beneath. The entire supporting structure of the tower is dragged down through the hole behind it like a tail.

TWENTY-SEVEN

I DROP THE DUFFEL BAG DOWN THROUGH THE JAGGED HOLE ONTO the third floor, where it lands in a hallway next to the hole going down through the center of the building, at the base of which rest the remnants of the tower structure and the collapsed cylinder of the tower itself. I climb down carefully, holding on to the top of an exposed wall and dropping next to the bag, losing my footing on the slippery surface and landing face first on the hallway floor, which is covered with several feet of water sloshing around and looking for a way down and out. I inhale some of the water, choking as I get to my feet. The only light in the hallway comes from the hole in the roof, so I keep one hand brushing on the side wall as I walk.

The building is not very wide, with one door at each end. I reach the door at the north end of the hallway after six strides. My hand closes on the doorknob; I try to turn it, but it's locked. I can feel the sloshing of the water vibrating along the soles of my feet. Too late; I sense another, more rhythmical beat: the footsteps of a runner. I see a blur of movement in my peripheral vision as I begin turning to my left, a huge shape barreling toward me and plowing into my midsection, slamming me through the door and shattering the frame.

I wrap my arms around his torso while we're still moving, twisting our bodies into a roll as he slams onto his back and slides several feet across the floor. He rolls over, onto his knees and back to his feet, surprisingly agile for his size. I close the distance as he reaches behind his back, retrieving an automatic pistol, but I reach him before he can aim it, leaping up on my last stride and connecting my knee with the base of his chin. His body slams backward, crushing halfway through a sheetrock wall as I fall on top of him. Using my left hand to prop up my upper body, I punch downward at his face with my right, the angle and gravity making the blows even more vicious. Within seconds, he goes limp.

As I'm getting the gun from the floor next to him a spray of dust peppers my face. It takes a fraction of a second for me to realize it's a gunshot. I fall sideways across the man's legs and fire the entire clip, fifteen bullets in all, in the

NOISE

direction of the doorway. A second figure, barely an outline in the dark, falls on top of the collapsed wooden door.

Most of the shots missed, but not all.

I quickly get back to my feet, walking in an arc toward the doorway, remaining out of view from the hallway until I reach the far wall of the room, creeping up to the door from the side. I take the second man's gun and step over his body and into the relative light of the hallway, where I can see a few feet ahead of me. Most of the water in the hallway has already found its way down, so the going is a bit faster and steadier, but I still keep one hand on the wall as I cross back, carefully picking my way around the hole in the floor.

As soon as I reach the door at the far end, I feel the impact in my upper chest, the force of the bullet propelling me backward and slamming me against the debris piled against the wall. The gun, knocked from my hand, skitters along the floor and over the edge of the hole to the lower level. My back is pinned against a section of the tower base. My chest burns white hot, the rest of me . . . ice cold.

The figure walks through the door holding a small gun, stepping gingerly along the wet, cluttered floor. Instantly I know it's him. His eyes smile. He looks even older in person, but his face has the same wild cruelty that I saw in the video as he raped my sister. Crooked teeth. Dead, brown eyes. Stained silk pajamas. A small gray rat of a man, with a filthy elegance that makes him all the more despicable.

"You're the brother," he says, standing above me and pointing the gun at my face. He squints at me, weaving his head every few seconds, as if trying to look around the falling snow.

I don't answer. My chest feels like it's exploding as I squirm against a wooden beam that's wedged against the wall, trying to angle my way upright.

"I almost don't want to shoot you again." His head bobs and weaves, almost comically now, and he swirls the gun in circles through the air, as if he's stirring a sideways pot. "You saw how much I liked your sister, poor girl. I can almost admire you. But family is a difficult thing, trust me . . . I know."

"Where is she?" I struggle to get the words out, a hammer inside pounding my chest.

"My sons are morons," he says, waving the gun from side to side now. "Both of them, I know. Your sister, too. They step in it, we clean it up. You and I, Mr. Leon. You and I. We're the cleaners. We're the real necessities." He seems to not even notice the hole in the roof, or the water pouring down through it.

"Where?" I ask again. I give up on the wooden beam and roll over onto my stomach, putting my hands flat on the wet linoleum. The cold water against my chest shrinks the pain into a tight circle, like a hand making a fist. Slowly, I pivot my legs sideways until I'm more or less on my knees. The change in vertical orientation causes an intense wave of momentary nausea to flow through me, nearly making me vomit. I stare down at the surface of the floor until the wave passes.

"It was that damn cop," the man says. "Had a thing for Vicky's wife . . . ah . . . your sister, whatever the fuck her name is, or was. You know they didn't have a warrant? I had it all covered." The Bear steps around me, lifting his head to the hole in the roof and briefly closing his eyes as snowflakes land on his face.

"I can't do business without rules, no different than the police, although not entirely the same either. Rastov?"

Closer now, I can see the deep crevices in his skin, days-old razor stubble growing out in multiple, conflicting directions, yellow and bluish-brown areas on his face and neck. I lean my shoulder against the wall and push up with my arms, sliding my body up against the wall with my palms until I'm standing in front of The Bear.

"Dead," I say, looking slightly downward at him now.

He tracks my movement closely with the gun, the smile gone from his face.

"Dead," I say again.

The Bear nods slightly, and then raises his chin in an odd, ugly gesture. "Well, as I said, a moron. I figured as much. But you can't choose family."

"Where's Lily?"

"Pretty cheap, I guess you know now, to buy a cop, eh? I own quite a few, as you've discovered. My little pets. By the way, I never knew you could break a safe like that," he says. "It was very interesting. We had a camera on you the whole time, streaming right into my living room. Too bad I was engaged in another room at the time and missed the live feed. Got to the recording a couple of hours later." He glances at the roof and then lowers his gaze back to me. "Yes. Very interesting."

"Where's my sister!" I move forward as I yell against the storm. His arm tracks my movement, the gun still pointed directly at my chest.

When I stop advancing, he doesn't move. Neither does the gun. "Where are the contents of my safe?"

"Everywhere," I say.

"No matter, Mr. Leon," he says, shaking his head and showing his stained teeth again. "You can publish them in *The New York Times*, for all I care, and I will still never see a day in prison. For all your success, you Americans still don't have the slightest understanding of how America works."

"I'm not American," I say.

"No, you wouldn't be now, would you?" His lips curl into a snarl.

"Lily," I say again.

"Yes, back to the girl. Well. Leon. You know what happens when you're transporting, say, I don't know, tomatoes?"

A large beam falls from the roof, crashing on the wooden floor and down through the hole next to him. He doesn't flinch. The entire building seems to be vibrating and resettling, but he continues. "And someone drops a box, and a tomato falls onto the floor and it splatters?"

I say nothing, my body shivering violently from the soaked clothes. I unzip my wool coat and let it fall to my feet on the floor, landing in a black, wet pile. My T-shirt is covered in blood, but the cold does help a little.

"Breakage," he says, raising the gun to my face and waving it back and forth in front of my nose. "We call it breakage." Another beam falls behind him, dragging a chunk of the tar roof with it.

"So, particularly and precisely," he says, still waving the gun, "I don't know where your sister is, any more than I'd know where the guts of the tomato would have been tracked to. Do you understand?"

"Someone must know," I say.

"Of course, Mr. Leon! Of course. Someone knows. The girl herself knows. But she's not telling little brother, eh?"

I don't catch what he says next. As his lips move, I feel the floor of the building shift a little, causing a slight rumble again. He looks up at the falling roof, which is finally caving in from the weight of the snow and loss of structural integrity. He raises both hands to protect his head, still holding the gun but no longer pointing it at me.

As the roof comes crashing down around us, I push off the wall with my foot and charge him. The handle of the duffel bag catches on my ankle and I veer to the side, off-balance. Dragging the bag behind me, I leap into the hole in the floor, just missing the largest part of the collapsing roof and grabbing his wrist as my feet clear the floor. We fall over the edge together, our bodies and the large duffel bag entwined, crashing through both floors and onto the concrete floor below. I cover up and roll into a fetal position as the roof crashes over us.

I don't know if it's age, or genetics, or just desperation, but my body takes the fall better than his does. I roll onto my knees and take the gun, still clenched in his hand, and struggle to get back to my feet. I stand above him and put the gun in my pocket. His eyes are open, staring toward the ground, and his mouth moves, strangely and rhythmically, like a fish gasping for air. I take a small flashlight from my side pants pocket and switch it on, but the lens is smashed from the fall.

I turn toward a table to look for another flashlight, but cannot see much of anything. My field of vision seems narrower than it should, causing me to pause and squint. As I make my way along the edge of the table, I feel his hands on my neck, his slight weight pushing me toward the wooden surface, the wound in my chest tearing in a fresh burst of searing, dizzying pain. It occurs to me that I've never thought of any downside to being deaf before, but having a murderous Russian criminal sneaking up on me, even an old weak soaking-wet one, could be the first.

He realizes his hands are not strong enough to strangle me, or that my neck is just too wide for a decent grip, so

NOISE

he lowers one hand to look for the gun. My hand closes on a curved metal hook of some sort lying atop the table. Something used to haul sides of beef, I think. As his hand reaches the grip of the gun, I drive my left elbow behind me, slamming it hard against his forehead. An instant later I'm pushing off the table with my hands and spinning around, swinging the hook in a wide arc as my body rotates toward him. The hook sinks deeply into the man's shoulder, nearly lifting him into the air. He falls against the wall with a look of shock as he stares down at the hook protruding from his shoulder.

I find my duffel bag near where we'd first fallen. Blood soaks the entire front of my body. An irrational anger burns inside of me now, seemingly directed at the pain in my chest, but the cold, rational voice inside of my head whispers otherwise. I reach inside of the bag and grab one of the Mason jars, lighting the rope wick with a match. I watch as the blue flame bulges out and creeps slowly down toward the base of the wick.

When I'm certain that the flaming wick has fully caught on, just before it reaches the surface of the metal lid, I throw the jar two floors up to the door where I first saw The Bear. Where he lives. Where he sleeps.

I want it all to burn.

TWENTY-EIGHT

THE SOUNDS I CANNOT HEAR: THE WHISTLE OF THE HAMMER AS IT arcs through the air; the wailing of pain and the begging of The Bear; the dripping of blood from thawing meat onto a wet concrete floor; the beautifully crude threats.

My own hideous voice.

I drag The Bear by the hook sunk through his shoulder into a walk-in freezer and toss his body into a corner on the floor. I stand above him, swaying, my blood mixing with the dead sludge staining the floor. Several minutes pass, me frozen in place, The Bear staring up at me like a wild, trapped animal. I am not a violent person. The American me has never yelled, has never until recently hurt another living being. I am mostly a vegetarian. I work hard. I read. I am everything the younger me could never have hoped to be.

But Rastov. The Bear. The police. Lily, Sara, South Carolina, Africa. All that changes are the clothes. I look down at The Bear one more time, trying to feel something other than hatred, but nothing comes of it. We're all animals, all of us . . . base.

I exit the freezer for a few seconds, and when I reenter, dragging the table behind me, The Bear is hard at work on the hook, trying to muscle it out of his shoulder with one hand, but the metal is sunk deep through the tendons. He tries several angles, but nothing works. Hope is adrenaline, fear masks pain, begging helps no one.

I yank him up by the hook and lay his upper body across the table, holding his hands outstretched, one at a time, as I nail his wrists to the wooden surface with large, square-cut nails. I put all of my 240 pounds behind the hammer, but even so, it takes several swings. His body shakes, the nails sink further into the wood, his face is pain. He may scream, but I cannot hear. And I do not care.

The building above burns a deep blue hue, collapsing in slow, fiery dance. A grave, for Lily, perhaps, or for me. Certainly for him.

The sound of the hammer into The Bear. The pain in his eyes. I have never seen so much hatred. It is beautiful to me, to reach this center, this uncomplicated base, to disassemble the past and honor a new history. It is another film, also homemade and rough, an overlay, an epilogue. The Bear is broken but I have spared his face, and to see those eyes, that is what I needed: to see his hatred flow into me, my own eyes sucking down the scum like bathtub drains. His life whirls into me and I taste the fear, the hope, the sharp sting of adrenaline pumping and the reeking muck of despair. His pain soothes me, a slow, thick poison. We will all die. But here, at this moment... I am young again. Here, once again, I understand the violence of life.

I imagine Lily watching me now, keeping score, making lists, balancing all. Is she shaking her head, sadly, at her broken avenger? Does the reckoning of her past bring her peace? Can she see? Will she hear? As a child from far away, she was the queen, ever more so than her mother. But she didn't survive. The world was not as we had imagined it to be, sister, not even close. The world is a cruel, bastard place, inhabited, every last inch, by predators and runners, Lily cold and lost somewhere, me hot and bleeding and swinging my hammer. Life as it is, not as we wish it to be.

The sounds I cannot hear: *The laughter of the watchers; the groan of my sister as The Bear cums inside of her, pulling her hair until the roots bleed.* The Bear screams and shits himself inside the dark freezer, adding to the cold sludge on the floor. *Lily's wailing and cursing and crying.* I scream at The Bear with all of my mighty, damaged voice, swinging the hammer at his ruined hands, hands that will never again touch anyone. *Lily at the end, beaten and pissed on and begging to die.*

Lily is dead. I am dead. It will never be enough.

I remove the stack of photos from my wallet that I'd printed at the Internet café a lifetime ago and place them facedown on the table in front of The Bear. They are small, about the size of playing cards. I draw an X on the back of the first photo and turn it over, laying it close to the pulp of his ruined hands and yanking his head up so he can see.

The Bear offers me anything I want. An animal can feel pain but cannot describe or transmit it adequately. The Bear both is and is not an animal. I lack hearing, so the Bear cannot transmit his experience to me unless I choose to see it. His pain is not my pain, but mine is very much his. I swing the hammer into his unhooked shoulder, and then I draw another X and flip another photo.

His lips move, frantically now, and I understand what he wants to know. *Five photos*.

On the back of the third photo, I write: *you are a rapist fucking pig*. I put the photo into the gristle of his hands and swing the hammer against the metal hook again. It's a sound I can feel.

Anything, The Bear mouths. He is sweating in the cold air of the freezer. Crying and bleeding and retching.

"I want my sister back!" I scream, swinging the hammer claw-side first into his mouth and leaving it there. His body shakes and twitches, flopping against the wooden table like a hooked fish.

I write a note on the back of his photo, holding it in front of his face, the handle of the hammer protruding from his jaw like a tusk. *You are number four.* There are a few seconds of space as the information stirs into him and I watch as he deflates, the skin on his face sagging like a used condom. He knows what I know.

I turn over the last photo for him. I lift it slowly and hold in in front of his face. Victor, his one good son, his *outside* accomplishment, his college boy, the one who tried to fuck him and they fucked my sister instead.

I remove another Mason jar from my bag, unscrewing the metal top and letting the thick fluid flow onto his chest and down his torso, watching as it seeps into his crotch, where it needs to be. I wipe my hands, slowly and carefully, and then I light a match, holding it in front of his face for a few seconds as the flame catches fully. He doesn't try to blow it out. He doesn't beg me to stop. He just stares at the match as the flame catches and puffs to size, his eyes following my hand as I drop it onto his chest.

The Bear shakes so hard from the pain that one of his arms rips from the table, leaving a skewer of meat and tendon on the metal spike. I lean into his ear, taking in his sweet reek and the rot of his bowels, and, in my own hideous voice, I say:

"Wait for me."

TWENTY-NINE

I SPEND SEVERAL MINUTES OPENING THE FRONT DOOR WITH THE big sledgehammer. Even from the inside, the door is very secure, steel set in concrete and keyed on both sides. I take out nearly half of the steel frame before it gives way and swings open. Outside, the snow is still blowing sideways, strong winds sweeping the accumulation into soft pillows against the side of the building.

I walk back to my truck, dragging the duffel bag the whole way. Stopping midway to look back, I can't tell that there's a fire, but I know it's there, and I know it will burn, slowly, from the inside out. The fire will creep up the walls, bleed sideways and engulf The Bear in a circle of heat.

I dump the duffel bag into the back of the truck, searching through the toolbox for a tube of Superglue. I squeeze what's left of the contents into the hole in my chest, wincing from the pain, and then I walk around to the front, not even seeing Jane until my hand is on the door handle.

"It's over, Leon," she says, pointing her gun at me for the third time. "Enough."

"No." I stand next to the door of the truck. "Not for me."

"Yes." The wind blows the snow sideways between us, swirling her hair underneath her chin.

"The files, Jane. They'll come out, sooner or later. It's a house of cards. Those above you will trade you in an instant."

"I don't care, Leon. I really don't." She lowers the gun and leans sideways against the rear quarter panel of the truck. The gun hangs by her side, her shoulders sag.

"Rico?"

"Stable," she says. "Doc says you saved his life, but he's not talking. I need to ask what you're doing here."

"How'd you find me?"

She nods sideways, toward the truck. "Hard not to."

I stare at her profile until her eyes turn to meet mine; hers deep and blue and penetrating, mine dark and flat, as always. "You need to let me go, Jane."

She tightens her coat against the wind, looking at my chest and noticing the wound for the first time. "You need—"

"I need to go." I squint against the snow blowing into my eyes.

"Look at you, Leon. You won't make it five blocks. You need to be in a hospital. It's over."

I start to open the door of the truck but she pushes back

against it with her arm, slamming it shut and turning into me as I reach behind my back and pull out the gun I took from The Bear. I push away from the fender and point the gun at her face.

"You saw the videos, Jane!" I scream the words against the howling wind, flinging them at her. "How could you just use people like that? How could you let that happen and do nothing?"

"Leon." She leans against the metal of the truck door, putting as much distance as possible between her face and the gun in my hand. "If I could have stopped that from happening I would have. You know that."

"I don't believe you!" I grab her coat in the fist of my left hand and throw her onto the ground, away from the truck.

"Get on your knees," I say. "Now."

"Leon, don't do this." She pushes her body up from the snow but stays on her knees, her face stiff with anger and defiance. "It won't help you find Lily."

"Where is she?" I shout.

Jane lowers her head. If she says something, I don't catch it.

"She was the only person I had in the world!" I press the barrel of the gun against her temple as she falls sideways into the snow. "Why couldn't you just leave her alone? She did nothing to you or the police! She had nothing to give you! NOTHING!"

"Leon. Don't do this. Please."

I hold the gun against her temple, the warmth of her

face melting the snow underneath her cheek. I pick up her weapon and aim it toward her car tires, firing until the gun clicks empty, then I throw the gun across the street, steadying myself with my other hand.

"Go fuck yourself, Jane." I kneel in the snow and whisper the words into her ears. I stare at her face for a moment longer and then grab the handle of the truck, pulling myself upright and entering the driver's seat.

I push in the clutch and start the engine, opening my window and looking at Jane lying next to the front tires, the big engine in the Dodge catching instantly and rumbling in the snow.

"Leon, wait," she says. "Please."

I put the truck in first, still holding the clutch down, and watch as she sits up.

"I'm sorry, Leon," she says, her face wet and reddened from the snow. "Neither of you deserved this. If I could have stopped it, I would have. There's nothing in the world worse than what they did to her."

"The line of people who hurt Lily," I say, turning away from her and facing the windshield. "It ends with me."

She struggles to her feet and stands next to the door. "And that's it, Leon? That makes it all better?"

"Goodbye, Jane," I say. I let out the clutch and the truck rolls away, leaving wide twin trails in the deep snow.

THIRTY

I DRIVE THE TRUCK BACK DOWNTOWN TOWARD TRIBECA, TACKING south and east along the smaller side streets, the truck sliding and slogging in the deepening snow. Some of the drifts come up higher than the front bumper, causing explosions of white powder as the truck crashes through them. There are no plows or salt trucks. No cars or pedestrians. No police. Just the swirling snow piling up against the cars and buildings, covering everything in sight.

I have these changing thoughts of Lily trailing in my mind as I slide through the dark streets of Manhattan. Of me rescuing her in a thousand different ways. In some, she's injured, tired, ashamed. In others, she's angry; she runs from me or tries to hit me. In yet others she's never left, still back in South Carolina, married with children, and me the quiet, doting uncle. Sometimes she's ill. In many, she's already dead. Always, she's lost.

I push these thoughts around in my mind like toys; when I ignore them, they simply reorder and present themselves in a slightly different way. Persistent. Stubborn. Enticing.

The truck rolls down the unplowed streets, churning and flattening the snow, making the ride soft and spongy, as if I'm rolling along a down comforter. The monster churning up the soft feathers and leaving behind soggy, used-up shreds.

For a few hours the snow will transform the city, covering up all the ugly parts, keeping the animals and the people hidden, stifling the noise and the clamor. Families will huddle inside and play cards by candlelight, their bodies pressed tightly together for warmth, never even knowing that it is the fear itself, the very desolation that they're trying so hard to push back, that is the source of their simple, temporary joy.

Tomorrow the snow will melt. The streets will become mud and slush, draining down the sewers and leaving behind only a film of salt and sand to mark the great storm. People will bundle up and go out in the vanishing snow, already losing one another, already forgetting their one night of peace and closeness.

They will curse the turning snow, reassure one another of how ugly and inconvenient it all is, of how it impacts their routines, of how it forces them to stop their work, to not watch TV. To huddle with their families and pets, hugging in the darkness, rationing their supplies but not, for once, their love, patiently waiting for the moment when they will be able to continue their lives.

How it costs them time, money.

The storm is a pause, a space, a vacation, an anomaly, a hole in their busy lives.

The lights will return. Candles will be stowed. Order restored. People will go back to work and school, the previous dark night of frightened politeness vanishing as the daily hatred of life creeps back into the messy spaces the storm left behind, and they will quickly forget the simple beauty of one another as briefly revealed by the storm.

But for now it remains dark. There is only me, only Leon; a ghost drifting through the storm in an ancient beat-down gray truck, looking for dead people or making them so.

I wish, just this once, that I could hear my own screams.

I stop the truck in front of the apartment building in Tribeca, the triangle below Canal Street, and stare up at the dark glass tower. The pain in my chest has eased somewhat, settling into a dull, steady ache, but I feel strange. Too numb. Hypothermia. Blood loss. Shock. PTSD. Sadness. Anger. Any number of calamities affect me.

A strange thought occurs to me as I open the truck door and step out into the deep snow, my legs feeling heavy and slow as I walk toward the building: I am far less of a criminal here, in this place and at this moment, than I ever was back in Africa. But the rules here are different. Here, the ones you save don't count. Here, the value of the victim is irrelevant.

Here, the punishment *is* the crime.

There are no footsteps leading up to the glass doors. No hardy city folk walking their little toy dogs. No lines outside of thumping nightclubs; no young, tired partiers hunched over coffees in all-night diners, feeding tomorrow's regrets. The city is closed tonight. There is only darkness. Only snow. Only Leon.

And one last stop to make.

THIRTY-ONE

I WALK UP THE SMALL SET OF CONCRETE STAIRS ENCIRCLING THE building, losing my footing several times on the slippery surface. By the time I reach the top of the stairs, I, too, am covered in snow. I stand in front of the glass wall and pull on the handles set into the twin glass doors, rattling the locks and pounding on the glass until I see movement inside, two flashlights bobbing side to side in the darkness. The twin cones of light sweep along the floor like low-hanging eyes on tired stalks, occasionally rising and hitting my own eyes before dipping back to the floor. A minute later two figures reach the door, shining the flashlights directly in my face. I can't see who is holding them from behind the glass, only that there are two of them.

I have no idea what they're saying, so I keep pulling on

the doors, shaking them with all my strength, but the locks hold tight.

I reach for my wallet, taking out the photo of Lily and flattening it against the surface of the door, slapping on the glass with the palm of my other hand and leaving small, bloody smears.

"My sister!" I yell.

One of the flashlights raps against the glass. The other one remains shining in my face. I can't see anything except the glare of the flashlights and my own face reflected in the glass, so I stare back at the light and keep pounding on the doors.

"Let me in!" I scream, my voice lost in the wind.

Both flashlights rise up to my eyes now. I slump against the door, my forehead hitting the cold wet glass and staying there. The flashlights drift to my chest, illuminating my thin, white T-shirt, soaked red with blood.

Some of the light reflects back inside now, to where I can just make out their faces. They're both young, black like me, probably sleepy and hateful of their jobs. Shaking their heads, laughing and pointing at my chest and bare arms shivering in the snow.

The flashlights recede and wink out after several minutes, letting the dark back in. Once my eyes readjust to the darkness, I can see the shapes of the two men walking away, shaking their heads, one of them slapping the other's back. Further inside the lobby there is some sort of dull emergency lighting lining the floor, so they don't need the flashlights there, but that light doesn't reach this far.

"Let me in," I say, more to myself than anyone, my head still resting on the glass. I stare at the two figures for several minutes, just barely able to make out the outlines of their bodies. They don't move. I don't move. The blood from my chest runs down the inside of my pants and into my boots, sticky and lukewarm, yet somehow comforting. Somehow, complete.

I turn around and walk back through the snow to my truck, taking slow, dragging steps and following my own bloody footprints, a map just for me. When I reach the back of the truck and open the tailgate, I take the hammer out of the bag and then the bag itself, slinging the handles over my left shoulder.

I start walking back to the building, planning to smash my way in through the glass, but after several steps, I stop. I stand there in the swirling snow, staring back up at the tall glass tower, dark and plastered with snow. Maybe it's the distance. Maybe it's the guards or Lily or Jane. Maybe it's just me. I've never been so tired in my life.

THIRTY-TWO

I WALK BACK TO THE TRUCK AND PULL MYSELF INTO THE DRIVER'S seat, laying the bag on the center console next to me and wincing from the ache in my chest. The entire seat is covered in my blood. I don't know how much I've lost. I don't even know how much I had to begin with.

I start the engine and press in the clutch, clumsily pulling the floor-mounted shifter down into second gear, then stomping down on the gas pedal and letting the clutch come up on its own. The truck slides sideways for a few feet before the big tires catch on the icy pavement beneath the snow, lurching forward suddenly and gathering speed. I shift into third and then fourth gear, letting the torque pull the truck back up the hill and watching in the rearview mirror as the building shrinks behind me. After a minute or so I slip the shifter back to neutral and slam on the brakes and the truck swings around 180 degrees in the snow, facing the building once more and rumbling softly in a cloud of white smoke from the exhaust.

It is very dark. The white snow on the road in front of me reveals the path like a dull, lighted runway next to the black buildings lining each side. The water on the hood of the truck shimmers with each revolution of the engine. I jam the gun into the rectangular hole in the dashboard where the radio would ordinarily have been, had I been born ordinary. The seat is cold and sticky, as are the steering wheel and the gear shifter, which helps with the grip.

I drop the truck back into second gear once more, stepping on the gas and letting my foot slip sideways off the clutch. My entire body screams to just go in the back seat and lie down. Briefly, I close my eyes. I think of Lily. The truck rockets down through the snow toward the glass building as I run through the gears, power-shifting and gathering speed.

Fifty miles an hour. Sixty. I stop looking at the speedometer, barely able to keep the truck in a straight line. It's too fast for the deep snow, and the decline of the road throws the truck off balance, causing it to snake from side to side and bounce off the other vehicles lining the narrow street, leaving a trail of broken mirrors and glass behind me.

But the truck keeps going. The building grows larger in the dirty windshield. A minute later, the big tires bounce up over the curb and then the small set of stairs leading up to the building. At the end of the stairs, the truck launches into the air toward the locked glass doors, remaining airborne as it closes the distance and slams into the sleek glass wall.

The truck hits the building going at least seventy miles an hour, obliterating the glass doors and much of the front façade along with them, leaving a trail of shattered glass and twisted metal. It bounces over a reception desk and several couches, crushing through two walls and an office of some sort before coming to rest inside a small Starbucks at the far end of the lobby.

I ram the truck door open with my shoulder, retrieving the gun from the dashboard and falling out of the truck and onto the tiled floor, landing hard on my hands and knees. My chest is bleeding freely again, the fresh blood soaking through my shirt as I pull on the door handle and lift myself to my feet. One of my eyes is covered in blood, dripping down from a gash on my forehead, but the other one works well enough. I walk around to the passenger side and work the bag free from where it's wedged in the foot well. My tools slosh around inside the bag, the Mason jars smashed and everything soaked with the thick gasoline mixture.

I sling the bag over my shoulder and hold the gun in front of me, walking back toward the reception desk in halting, uneven steps. I stop halfway across the lobby and turn around, looking back at the truck one last time. I don't know why, but it makes me sad to see it like this, broken and stuck and sagging on bent wheels, hissing air, leaking liquids. For years, the old truck had been my only friend, the only thing in my life, in a messy, cruel world, to never let me down.

Tomorrow it will be surrounded by crime scene tape before being hauled off and crushed for scrap. The lobby will be cleaned and repaired. I will be dead.

THIRTY-THREE

THE WIND FROM THE STORM OUTSIDE BLOWS THE SNOWDRIFTS onto the lobby floor as I walk toward the desk. One of the security guards rushes out, charging for me but slipping on the wet marble and falling into my chest. The pain is excruciating. I yank him back by his hair and push him to the floor, aiming the gun at his head.

I have no idea if there are any bullets left. If it were an empty revolver, you could tell that from the front, so long as you weren't completely terrified by the sight, which any normal person would be. But an automatic doesn't have those visuals. There is just a barrel. And a trigger. The bullets are hidden, stacked in the handle and waiting to be shot.

"Call the other guard," I say.

The guard doesn't answer, turning his head away to avoid looking at the gun.

"I have no reason to hurt either of you," I say. "But I will."

I can't see his lips. I can't tell if he's talking or not. He just stares at the floor in front of his face.

"Give me your phone," I say.

He looks up at me, finally, his face young and scared.

"Your phone," I say again.

He reaches into his pocket, pulls out an iPhone and holds it out to me. I take it in my left hand, drop it to the floor and stomp it to bits with my boot, never taking my eyes off his.

"The other guard," I say again.

Just as I'm about to say something else the other guard appears from behind the crushed remnants of the reception desk, popping his head up like a dashboard toy.

"The fuck is with you!" He stares at the snow in the lobby, then back to the truck, and then back to me, seeming half amused and half panicked. To young Americans, everything is a movie.

I wave the gun at him sideways, motioning him to come over. He hesitates for a second, and then walks to my side of the desk, keeping the other guard between us. I like that he's not too scared. Frightened people do stupid, dangerous things.

"Phone," I say.

"Come on, man." He stares at me defiantly. "What the fuck?"

NOISE

I pick up the large rectangular desk phone, presumably from the reception counter but now scattered on the floor, and hold it in front of my eyes. I can't tell if there's a dial tone, but a light blinks on the console, so I throw the whole unit back to the floor and crush it with my boot, stomping down until the center flattens and the blinking light goes dark.

"I won't ask again," I say, turning back to the second guard.

He reaches into his pocket and takes out another iPhone, dropping it on the floor and crushing it with his own boot.

"OK?"

I nod. "Victor Igzoi," I say.

"Building's evacuated," the first guard says, still crouched on the floor. "All of downtown is."

The second guard answers without the slightest hesitation. "Sixteen-B," he says.

"Elevators?"

He shakes his head, smiling. "Storm, man. Have to huff it." He stares at my blood-soaked shirt, his expression indicating his doubts that I'll reach it.

I look down at the first guy on the floor. "Up," I say, waving the gun.

"You gonna shoot us?" the second guard asks.

I ignore the question. "Where's the bathroom?"

He points to the corner next to the destroyed Starbucks. "I think you crushed it."

"Walk," I say, pushing them toward the truck.

When we reach the truck, I secure their hands to the rear bumper with plastic cable ties. The ties are slick with gasoline, but I manage to secure them well enough. The two guards don't resist, and if they're talking, I can't tell.

I reach into the back of the truck and get a wool blanket, dropping it at their feet.

"You're fucking crazy, dude," the skinny, taller guard says.

"Stairs," I say.

He points to a doorway next to the elevator bank and I start walking.

I walk through the heavy door into the stairwell, dumping the contents of the duffel bag onto the first-floor landing, and then walk back out toward where the reception desk was. After searching through a few crushed drawers, I find a clipboard with a few sheets of paper and a pen. I take both.

Back inside the stairwell I pick up a handful of the square nails and the small sledgehammer from the floor where I emptied the bag and walk back down to the stairwell door. I hammer a single sheet of paper onto the outside of the door with one word. It reads: BOMB.

I nail the door shut and walk back up to the landing and grab the fire ax from the floor. I pocket the small sledgehammer and throw the soaked duffel bag down the stairs and I start climbing, pulling myself up using the rails bolted to the wall. When I reach the second floor I pull out my Zippo, light it and drop it through the gap between the stairs. The bag catches instantly and the hallway erupts in deep blue and yellow flames.

The hallways and the door itself are fireproof, but between the heat and the nails and the sign, if the cops do show up, maybe I've bought myself some time. About the time it takes me to drag myself up sixteen flights of stairs, pulling myself with my arms each step of the way.

THIRTY-FOUR

THE RELATIVE HEAT INSIDE OF THE BUILDING MAKES ME FEEL queasy, forcing me to stop on each landing to rest. Each time I sit on the stairs it takes me that much longer to pull myself up again. My chest thumps with every beat of my heart, my vision becoming narrower until I have to swivel my head to see anything. Leon. Deaf and blind.

I reach the sixteenth floor and fall through the fire door, landing hard on my side and staying there for several minutes, panting for breath. The hallway is lined along the floor with dull red emergency lights, barely illuminating the apartment doors lining each side of the hallway. I walk unsteadily along the narrow hallway, using my arm to wipe the blood from my eyes as I slide against the wall. I stop in front of each door for several seconds, staring until I can make out the letters, counting down from *M*.

When I reach 16B, I lift the heavy ax, its handle slippery from a mix of gasoline and blood, and spin around, swinging at the lock and screaming in pain. The door collapses inward on the first swing, and I fall inside.

The narrow entryway of the apartment leads into a massive living/dining room combination lined with floor-to-ceiling windows overlooking downtown Manhattan, the East River and, beyond that, Brooklyn. Victor is sitting at a table with his back toward me and staring at the glass wall, a gun resting next to a glass of amber liquid and a bottle. I recognize him easily from the video: a stooped, weak man.

I walk right up to him and press the gun against the back of his head.

"Better you," he says sadly, staring at me in the reflection of the glass wall of windows, "than my father."

"Where is Lily?" I imagine my voice as calm and even inside my head. When he doesn't answer, I pick up the gun from the table next to his glass and fire into the giant windows, leaving ten holes before the gun clicks empty. It's a heavy, serious gun, at least a .45, but the thick, storm-grade glass absorbs them.

"Where is she?" I scream, my face inches from his head.

As he reaches for his glass I drag him upright and against the side wall of the room, punching him until my arms weaken and he falls to the floor.

NOISE

I step over his body and grab the table, lifting it above my head and slamming it back down to the floor until the legs break off. I drag the table back across the floor to the front of the apartment, opening the door and hammering another note onto the outer surface, same as the one in the lobby. Then I close the door and wedge the table under the inside doorknob, removing the small sledgehammer from my side pocket and securing the broken table to the oak floor with the few nails I have left.

With each swing, I scream from the pain in my chest.

When I return to the main room, Victor hasn't moved from the floor, where he lies beaten and drunk. I throw the hammer across the room, shattering the big window and letting the storm rush in. This high up, the wind is much stronger, knocking over papers, a magazine stand and other light items as the room fills with the swirling snow.

I drag Victor upright and over to the window and push him up against the wall next to where the window was just seconds ago, one of his feet slipping over the edge into the empty blackness. With my other hand I reach behind me, retrieve Rico's gun from my waistband and push the barrel into his chest.

"Lily's dead," he says, finally looking at me, his face swollen and sagging.

"Where is she!" I scream the words into the wind.

"You're the brother," he says. His eyes are calm, and oddly kind. "She told me you'd come."

"Tell me where she is."

"She had nothing to do with this." He shivers and looks down through the window to the street far below. "It was all a fucking setup. She didn't know anything. Just that I was going to testify. It was all arranged. Part of the deal was that she'd know nothing, to protect her. We would have been across the country by now, in witness protection. She was a good person." He's crying now, staring at the street below. "She made me a better person."

"And?"

"And," he says softly. "I recanted. To protect her." He looks old and tired. Beaten by more than just me. "But they took her anyway. They made me watch."

"They're dead," I say.

"Who's dead?"

"Everyone." I look down at the street below with him, blue and white flashing lights visible in the distance, a trail of police vehicles slowly following a sanitation truck plowing a path through the deep snow.

Victor starts crying freely, his shoulders shaking. "She died for nothing. I wasn't going to testify."

"No, asshole," I say. "She died for you. For a weak piece-of-shit nobody like you."

I drag his body fully upright and turn him around so he's facing me with his back to the howling storm. We both sway in the wind, balancing on the edge of the floor as the flashing lights reach the base of the building.

Without warning, he starts screaming over my shoulder with a wild, desperate energy. "Get back!" He pushes against me, bucking and squirming, nearly causing me to lose my balance and both of us to go sailing through the window. "Get back in your room!" He's wild-eyed, spraying my face with saliva.

I swing him around sideways, still holding his shirt bunched in my fist, so his back is toward the main room, and I swing the gun over his shoulder, my fading vision focusing on a small child standing in the hallway off of the living room.

Victor struggles against my grip, forcing me to take a step backward, closer to the destroyed window, to regain my balance. "Don't," he pleads. Tears run down his cheeks as he twists around to see the girl. "Please, don't."

"Who is that?" I scream, grabbing his hair and yanking his face back to mine so I can see his words. "Who the fuck is that?"

"Please!" he says. "Get back in your room, Lucy! Everything's fine!"

The girl doesn't listen, instead walking around me and clinging to Victor's leg, both of them balancing near the missing wall of glass. The gun drops out of my hand and clatters off the edge of the floor, falling sixteen stories to the icy ground below.

"Please," he says again. "Please, Leon. She loved you."

I release my grip on Victor and drop down to my knees,

landing heavily on the floor and staring at the little girl. She looks just like Lily did when I first met her, so many years ago, at JFK International Airport.

The girl speaks to me, half hiding behind Victor's leg but ignoring his pleas. "Are you here to find my mother?"

I grab Victor's pant leg and drag him away from the ledge. He falls gently backward, landing in a sitting position a few feet into the room.

The wind howls into the apartment. The girl stands directly in front of me as I kneel before her, centered in front of the broken window, balanced only by the wind. I turn sideways and glance down at the street below, watching as the police form a barrier with their cars and advance toward the building, crouch-walking in the snow. The girl reaches up and touches my face, crying, but her eyes remain wide open.

"Mommy said someday," the girl says to me. "Mommy said you'd come, someday."

I lean against the edge of the wall and sit down, landing hard on the floor with my left leg dangling over the edge.

"You're Leon," she says, touching my face with her small, shaking hands, caressing me as a blind person would. I watch her as she studies my face. Her eyes, Lily's eyes. I stare, transfixed, at her strength, and, for the first time in many years, I truly remember my sister. The girl looks away, briefly glancing at the missing window as if seeing the hole for the first time, and then swings her gaze back to me. In my failing, fading vision, it's like seeing the sun emerge after a long, dark storm.

The last thing I see, the fire in her eyes, her small hand against my cheek, her lips, moving softly, her words:

"You're Leon. You're the lion that eats the bear."

EPILOGUE

DETECTIVE JANE REINHART SIGNS ME OUT FROM THE DOWNTOWN station on a Tuesday at 7 a.m., a few days after my final hearing. The same guard who served dinner the previous night cuffs my hands behind my back and processes me out, walking me down the wide, gray hallways. My legs are soft. I'm tired. The other inmates watch as I pass their cells, each nodding in turn.

Near the front of the building, the guard steers me into a small side room where the two detectives are waiting. Neither looks at me as the guard removes the chains from my wrists and ankles. High on the wall is a vertical-slit window. There's no sun, but I look up anyway.

When I turn back to face them I see the same small smile on Jane's face that she wore as she testified at my hearing, initially against me, finally for me. A smile of sadness, of regret, of resignation. She turned out to be a friend after all.

But as soon as I see her face, the crooked downturn of her lips; as soon as our eyes meet, I know.

"DA says you'll probably do ten," Rico says, without his usual smugness. "Maybe less. Your testimony helped. And they'll segregate you. You'll be all right." Jane touches the edge of the metal table, tapping her fingers as if playing on an imaginary piano. The room is small and gray, lit from above by a fluorescent tube covered in grime.

"Don't kill anyone else," he adds.

"You won't do ten." Jane finally looks at me. I know they can't understand the deaf world, only the deaf and blind can, but I've done my time. Prison is just another quiet room.

Rico looks at his phone. Jane hands me my pad and marker, and the instant our hands touch her smile fades.

"There's something you need to see," she says, her eyes burning with sadness. "Are you ready?"

I nod, and Rico takes my arm, leading me out of the station, down to a sedan in the basement garage. Sitting in traffic, Rico makes small talk, asking if I've followed baseball. I haven't. Jane asks me if I want anything to eat. I don't. In the rearview mirror, her eyes ask me if I'm all right.

I'm not.

Outside, through the tinted windows of the car, the sky

is dark, thick with rain and cold. I watch as the streets of Manhattan streak by in a blur, everyone hurrying somewhere, wrapped up like fleeing mummies, cursing the inevitable weather and instinctively avoiding one another. Lives carefully planned, yet poorly executed.

The newspapers called me The Silent Angel. The prosecution called me a coldblooded killer. The court-appointed lawyer pleaded with me to go to trial. Maybe partly for her career, but I think she genuinely believed it was the right thing to do. I didn't care either way, and I still don't, but it was Jane who convinced me to testify and take a plea deal. I did exactly what I was accused of, no more and no less. She testified against me on the evidence, but for me on character and circumstance. She pushed until her own official reprimand, and then, suddenly, it was over. I am a felon. Lily is gone. The last question the prosecution asked me was if I had then or have since regretted my actions. My lawyer objected before I could answer. Later, in private, Jane asked me again, and I answered.

Rico stops the car in front of a Starbucks downtown and goes in for coffee, irritated at Jane's request.

"Take your time," she says. "Get it right. Three black, some muffins." When he leaves, she exits the car and climbs in next to me, pushing me forward and unlocking the cuffs. I rub my wrists to get the blood flowing again, and she grabs my chin and turns my face toward hers, inches away.

"You always hear about this from the lifers, the one case

so totally and completely unfair that you spend your life drinking it away. I'm getting so fucking old," she says. I turn to look out the window, but she pulls my face back toward her.

"What you did to those men is sick, Leon. It's wrong. But I wonder, sometimes. I wonder if I had been your sister, if I had been Lily, would I have wanted to see you stopped? I can't answer that." She shakes her head slowly and looks out the front window. "I can't answer that question and still be a cop. But sometimes I just want to. Sometimes, I wish I could be a woman who had the courage to answer that question."

"You are," I say to her. "You are."

Across the street, families line up for the ferry to the Statue of Liberty. The statue of freedom. The statue of justice, of opportunity, of renewal, of second chances. They line up for photos and candy. Impatient children, lost lovers, dutiful policemen and women, hawkers and punks on the sidelines selling memories, the gears of life silently grinding us all toward the same quiet defeat. Any one of them could be me. Or Lily. But I could never be them. There are lines you cross, and you never see them again.

There's a theory that the deaf never leave the womb. That there is a part of us that never comes out. That if we were ever to hear the world, we would implode at the onslaught, that we exist, our entire lives, insulated and isolated, as we were, at the very beginning. Someday, they will cure us, and we will be gone, wiped from the earth. I have no reference point for imagining what that may be like, but I've never wished for sound. I never wished for inclusion, never explored empathy.

I don't regret. I don't even understand the word.

Jane still holds my pad and pen in her lap, her fingers making small circles on the blank page. "It's a long line in there," she says, her lips moving slowly. Her hair is unkempt, curling under her chin. She is a beautiful woman. Like Lily. Like Sara. Not like me.

"Why didn't you just run? No one wanted to chase you, but you sat there. You waited. I don't get it, Leon. After everything, you just sat there. You could have gotten away."

She tries to take my hands, but I pull them back and reach for the pad instead. Part of me wanted to run, and still does.

In my pad I write *Lucy*, and tear off the sheet for her. She crumples it in her fist and looks out the far window.

"This is all wrong, Leon," she says, but I can tell she doesn't believe it. "You should have run."

The sun peeks out over the water behind us. *No*, I write again.

"OK," she says. "Can I ask you something then?"

I nod.

"If you had found her alive, would you have stopped?"

I consider the question for a minute or so, the same question I'd been asking myself all week and purposely not answering. I stare out over the water at a barge crossing the calm, flat waters of the bay, past the cloud cover toward the open ocean beyond the city. The world just keeps moving.

Finally, as Rico makes his way back to the car with the bag of coffee and food, I look back toward her face, remembering the same strength, the same defiance, that I saw in Lily when we were children, so long ago.

Rico enters the driver's seat, and the weight of the car shifts to accommodate him. He hands Jane the two paper cups of coffee and waits.

I write my answer and turn the pad to her. *No. I would not have stopped. I would never have stopped.*

She hands me a coffee and a muffin from the bag, returns the pad to me and opens the door, but I stop her. I write again and turn the pad for her to read. *I cannot live in that world.* She stays in the back seat and taps Rico on the shoulder, signaling him to drive, but he doesn't.

While she is still holding the pad, I write *I am ready to see her now.* Jane leans forward and rests her head against the back of the seat in front of her. *That's why I'm here?* I write. I drop the pad in her lap and turn toward the window.

She exits the car and returns to the front passenger seat. My hands are still uncuffed. The door is unlocked. The sun begins to emerge from behind the clouds, shining over Battery Park and the waters beyond.

"Did you ever think she was still alive?" Jane asks from the front seat. Rico blows on his coffee and puts the car in drive.

NOISE

I shake my head and stare through the window, remembering my mother crying at the funeral, shortly before her own death. I write: *Lily died years ago.*

We emerge from the elevator to the basement of the hospital and walk down another long gray corridor, Jane and Rico flanking me. I don't feel like a prisoner, at least no more than I've ever been, but as the doctor approaches, Rico cuffs my hands again, in front this time.

"Sorry," he says.

I nod and walk with them into the bright, cold room.

Lily lies on a silver metal table covered with a white sheet, crisp and unwrinkled. From her shape alone, somehow, I know it's her. It's odd to see her like this, years later, frail and childlike, still innocent, peaceful in a way I'd never seen her before. I try to block out the flashes from the video. I try to see her as she was.

"Suffocation," the doctor says. He's old and gray and seems kind. "She didn't suffer at the end, but her body shows signs of severe and prolonged—"

Jane stops him in mid-sentence with her hand, and he steps back. Rico steps back as well, leaning against the door but staying inside. I am, after all, a dangerous man.

In my pad, I write: *Can I touch her?*

Jane nods.

I lean in slowly and kiss her forehead, and then I lay my head on her chest, as I did countless nights as a child. But there is no heartbeat to soothe me, no slow breaths to surf.

There is no more Lily. After a few minutes, Jane touches my arm and nudges me up. I wipe the tears from my eyes and turn to face her.

I write: *The video?*

Jane takes my hand in hers. "No one will ever see that," she says. "It's over, Leon." I don't want to cry in front of them, but I can't help it. For the first time I feel relieved. I feel ready.

"There's something else," she says. "Something you should see."

Jane lifts Lily's hand and turns it over, revealing a fresh scar on her wrist. It's crude, but I recognize it.

"The doctor says it was done by hand, shortly before she died, maybe by one of the other girls. A sharpened ballpoint pen. Hence the infection."

I don't say anything.

"It's too shallow," she says, filling the space. "The scars would have faded away in time."

For the first time, I notice the cold air in the room, and I breathe it in as deeply as it will go.

"Do you know what it means? Is it some kind of message?"

The air chills me, curling into my lungs and around my own heart, threatening to freeze me, and I let it.

"Leon?" Jane's hand falls onto my arm and stays there.

I lean forward once more and kiss my sister on the forehead, my tears landing on her cold, pale cheeks.

"Leon?"

NOISE

I stand up to my full height and turn away from Lily and toward Jane. In her hand is my marker.

The cold sinks into the center of my body and stays there.

"Do you know what it means?" Jane asks again.

I feel cold and peaceful, not quite human, but strangely alive. I nod once. I take the marker from Jane's hand and look at Lily one last time. This is how I will remember her. In my pad, I write: *It's the first word she taught me in sign language. Before we learned the real symbols, we had to make up our own. She made me memorize it when I was still a child, sitting in the bathroom with the shower on hot all the way, watching as she drew on the wet glass of the mirror with her finger.* I see the symbol and the word clearly in my mind, dripping down the wet glass and fading in the thick steam, Lily making me promise to remember, every night the same, making me promise.

Jane looks at me, patiently waiting.

I smile and then I take her hand in mine and turn it over, the marker in my right hand. I write the word on the soft white skin of her wrist, in small, clear block letters. I write carefully. I write boldly. I write with peace, with hope and with resignation. On her skin, I write:

HOME.

AFTERWORD

I'd never imagined myself writing a novel. Novelists have long and fully mystified me. Black magic, to me. And for much of my writing life, I've had a special disdain for writers who insist that it's easier to write a novel than a short story. After all, it takes me years to finish a twenty-page story, and at that rate, it's little more than a hobby. I'd spend a decade of my life just writing the first draft.

I wrote *Noise* in around 4 months. Deep into my second novel now, I believe I finally understand what they meant. Writing a novel circumvents the always-on editor present in all writers. When you start writing a novel, you know you're going to throw most of it away. You know it's crap. You know, in the beginning, that it sucks especially badly, that abandoning this weak, alien fledgling, sprung forth from your softest innards, is a front-row certainty, and that's OK. You just have to write it, scene by blind scene, because you're building something bigger than your mind is accustomed to looking at. That's what you've decided to do, so you do it.

Someone who writes short stories is a writer. A novelist is, first, a reader. Then an archaeologist, a habitual explorer. You pick a place and decide to dig. And dig. Your map is only so big, drawn by a blind idiot. You see the next day. The next minute. That is all. You give up control. You give up knowing. You're not the star. The story is the star. Your characters are the stars. You're nobody. The novelist allows the curiosity to take center stage.

The novelist, in essence, gives up on writing, and he or she decides to tell a story instead. The editor has nothing to do until the story is written down. He sits in a corner and waits until you tell him there is something to chew on. Something to tear at. If you can ignore him long enough, you'll finish. You can't hold an entire novel in your mind; nor can he. You have to write it down just to see what happens. So you willingly trade a few months or years of your life to dig that hole. You build a camp around that hole. You create strong characters to help you dig. You fortify your camp against the editor. You make sure enough of you survives to complete the task.

Halfway though your novel, you're no longer a writer sitting alone in the woods. You have a team. Imaginary or not, you have a team. You're the manager, the facilitator, the enabler, the executioner.

When I sit down to write a short story, I already know what will happen, and how long I have to make it happen. A novel is a leap of faith. Too big for any one person. Certainly, too big for me. That is, I think, what those writers meant. Writing a short story is like diving into a lake looking for that beautiful fish that's always eluded you. Until and unless you find it, you're drowning. Writing a novel, however, is like grabbing the fin of a whale and holding on until the very end. If you knew where the whale was going, you wouldn't need to write the novel. But if you didn't start the novel, you'd never have found the whale.

Although I truly believe anyone can write one, it is a difficult task. Not so much the actual writing itself, but the necessary vacuum that being a writer creates in your life. You cannot be an observer and a participant at the same time. You really do have to choose, and I think that's where we fail. We isolate ourselves, we drink, we dive inward because we really don't get what the fuss is about. All the while, the words burn holes in us.

Persevere, however, and you will be astounded at the resources that come to your side. And so, a few people to thank. Jim Thomsen, my editor, who brazenly ignored my repeated attempts to lengthen this book and chopped away like a madman. He's the buzz cut of editors, brutal, and brutally effective. Any errors in the final product are a result of my stubborn meddling subsequent to his wizardry. I recommend him highly. Pete Garceau for his brilliant cover art. Morgana Gallaway for the beautiful and exacting interior work. Beth Jusino, book-marketer extraordinaire. Without her insight, knowledge and planning, it's unlikely that you'd have even seen this book. And the rest of the folks at The Editorial Department—you are the essence of professionalism. Leina Bektassova, for working with me on the story concept and early drafts; for encouragement, support and, when needed, a good ass-kicking. Andrea Cabrera for editing the final drafts. Luray Hodder, who was with me from the beginning. Her first words to me: "I'd never date a writer, but we could be friends." So it began. She lived long enough to see my first publication, and I am honored to be among those around the world who miss her dearly.

Last, my sister Melanie. She's the busiest person I've ever known. I have never seen her not work for more than 30 minutes at a time, and yet she took the time to read the early drafts of *Noise*. I remember years back, during a discussion concerning social hierarchy, she asked me if there were any people in the world whom I admired. At the time, I had to think quite hard to come up with a single name. Ask me today, however, and the answer is quite simple. Her.

To all others, thank you for taking the time to read my work.

A sneak preview of Brett's new book, **Ren**, coming in 2015:

REN

BY BRETT GARCIA ROSE

ONE

Akron, Ohio. 9 P.M.

Ren knew the woman would be dead from the moment she sat at the table across from him. It's in the way they approach, he thought to himself as he watched her enter the diner through the glass door. The way they move and turn. Two steps forward, one back, always hesitating, always thinking. The ones who run, the ones who survive, they don't rely on thought. They live on muscle memory. They live on momentum. They never look back.

"Ren?" she asks, sliding into the booth and removing her hands from thick, wool mittens. The woman is slight, with big eyes and thick red hair, mid-forties but looks older.

Ren nods, sliding a thick envelope across the table in front of her. "10K, circulated. Passport, stamped and circulated. Denver driver's license renewed three times, six points against. Two credit cards, $700 each. One burner cell, sealed."

"Are you sure these will pass for real documents?" she asks.

"Ma'am," Ren says. "These are real documents."

The woman sighs and puts both hands around the coffee cup in front of her. "So that's it? You take me now?"

"No," Ren says. "There's a blue Mustang parked out front. You passed it when you walked in. Your first address is on a typed note inside the passport. Drive the Mustang there tonight, and then leave it at the airport in the morning. After you land in Montreal eat what you need to inside the airport, and use the automated check-in at the hotel directly to the south of the international terminal. Turn on the phone at 6 a.m. the following morning. A text message will be waiting; confirmation for either another flight or a car rental. Memorize the confirmation number, destroy the phone and leave immediately."

Ren sips his coffee as the woman leafs through the items in the envelope.

"Where am I going after Montreal?"

"I don't know that," Ren says. "I'd be either dead or out of business if I did. Did you bring the items I requested?"

The woman hands over a white purse and goes back to sipping her coffee. Ren looks inside, noting the phone, wallet, makeup kit and other items a woman would normally carry on a short drive.

REN: coming 2015

"My children?" the woman asks.

"Second stop," Ren says, staring at her face. "And change your appearance as soon as you leave this diner. Walmart. Different clothes, scissors for your hair, dye, cosmetic contacts. You should have done this already. Lucky for you Halloween is coming."

"How do you know I didn't already?" She asks, a shy, nervous smile on her face. "Change my appearance, I mean."

Ren stares at her, his expression blank. "If you did, you'd be touching your hair, glancing at the mirror behind me, getting used to your new self."

"They said you were good."

"I'm alive," Ren says, finishing his coffee and standing up to leave.

"Wait," she says, putting her hand on his forearm. "Please, just for five minutes."

Ren hesitates for a moment, looking around the empty diner, and then settles his weight back into the vinyl booth.

He motions to the waitress, two fingers, asking for more coffee. They say nothing until their cups are refilled and the waitress returns to the front counter.

"What about my car?" she asks.

"There will be an accident by the time your flight lands in Canada," he says.

"With a body?" she asks, staring straight at him.

"Three," he says. "Burned. Takes a few days to identify dental records."

"Everyone told me not to fly," she says, staring at the cup on the table in front of her. "Said it was the worst thing I could do."

Ren stares at her for a moment. "If you ever have the law after you, then yes. But not here. Not the people looking for you. After 9/11 it's a lot harder to get live flight records. These guys are good, but not technical enough. They'll keep looking for you, though."

"For how long?"

"Forever."

The woman considers this for a moment, and then nods.

"You can never look back," he says, reading her mind.

"I know," she says. "Believe me."

"I don't believe anyone," Ren says. "No contact at all. No old friends. No new friends. No Facebook, e-mail, nothing, not even the Internet itself. Don't become somebody else. Become no one. If anyone from your past contacts you, and I mean anyone, be ready to run in five minutes. And that $10K in the envelope? Make sure that's always replenished. Always ready. That's your lifeline. From now on, that money is as important to you as air."

"You've done this before?" she asks.

"Many times," he says.

"No, I mean . . . once."

Ren hesitates, not wanting to answer, but the expression on her face weakens his resolve. "Yes," he says. "Once. Long ago."

"And the people looking for you? They never caught up?"

"No," he says, standing up to leave. "The people who were looking for me are all dead."

She grabs his arm as he stands. "Wait," she says. "Can you do that for me?"

"No," he says, leaving four dollars on the table for the coffee and tip. "But ten thousand dollars can buy you a lot of things."

"OK," she says, setting her jaw and staring up at him. "OK. Any last advice?"

"Yes," he says. "When you reach the second stop, and the termination of our arrangement, you'll feel safe. You'll be tempted to stay. To rest. Don't. Get as far away as you can. Keep running."

TWO

Quantico, Virginia. 8 A.M.

"He's not involved," Agent Victoria Wilson says, cutting off the man standing in front of the conference table with his back to her.

Special Agent Vince Mark, her direct superior, stares at the glass wall of the quiet room, waiting for Wilson to continue.

"Sir, he does one, maybe two jobs a year, low-level disappearances. Lives in a trailer with three wheels in the mountains of upstate New York," she says. "He works alone, takes jobs based on some weird personal criteria."

"You've seen this trailer?" Mark asks, sitting across the conference table.

"Photo, once," Wilson says. "He moves it around."

"On three wheels?"

"He jacks it up high, sir," Wilson says. "He's handy, what can I tell you?"

"So, he was contacted."

"Yes," Wilson says. "Single phone contact. Less than one minute. And even if that was long enough, he won't go for it. He doesn't do retrievals. Doesn't interact with military. And detests Homeland Security."

"Sounds like a wonderful guy," Mark says, raising one of his bushy gray eyebrows. "But a man like that has some sort of honor code. They all do. An old friend needs help, for all you know he's already on the job."

Mark leafs through the papers in a folder on the table in front of him, chewing on the back end of a pen. "Leverage?"

"Sir, he won't do it," she says. "Definitely not with Homeland Security attached. And if he was on it, there would be no press, no kidnapping, nothing. Not his style."

Mark takes a sip of water from a plastic bottle on the table in front of him, taking the extra time to screw the cap back on. "So we don't tell him," he says, replacing the plastic bottle on the table. "Put him on the girl's trail. Say she's one of his projects getting repossessed."

"Sir," Victoria says. "He'll know. And even if he doesn't, he won't care."

The third person in the room, Joe Barber, also the most junior, speaks for the first time. "He has a niece in New York. Same school as our Vic."

"He's worked for us before?" Mark asks, ignoring the interruption.

"Not directly," Wilson says, glaring across the table at Barber.

"Explain?"

"Wit-sec has specific protocols," Wilson says. "Very few people qualify. So his name is made available through intermediaries. Citizens avail themselves. Outside of our purview."

"Agent Barber," Mark says, looking directly at the junior agent for the first time. "You'll accompany Wilson to New York. Get on the niece. Same school—maybe they know each other. Use that. If he refuses to get involved, involve him."

"Yes, sir," Barber says, avoiding eye contact with his partner as their boss stands up.

Mark pauses at the door and addresses Wilson, ignoring the junior agent again. "No H.S. for now. You two will report only to me."

"Sir," Wilson says, "you don't want to do this. He's unpredictable at best. We can't control him."

He answers without turning. "We don't have to, Victoria. You've said it before: he already works for us. It's just another job to him."

She answers as the door closes behind her boss. "No, sir. It isn't."

THREE

West Village, Manhattan, N.Y. 1 A.M.

The concert begins at 12 a.m. in a small, crowded lounge on Bleecker Street. The sole performer wears a simple white dress, sitting upright behind a scratched grand piano, her strong vocals alone filling the dark room before the piano begins. Ren stands at a bar at the opposite end of the room, sipping a draft beer and watching the young woman sing.

He watches her often, more frequently than she knows. And she's good. The room remains still and silent as she performs her music, songs she's been composing for as far back as Ren can remember. The room watches her, entranced. Ren watches the room, wary.

In Ren's world, life can explode at any moment, but this particular routine has been going on for years. During the

REN: coming 2015

break Ruby Stone talks to everyone, working the room, as Ren adjusts his position to avoid her. There's little reason to; Ren is always cautious, but old habits die hard.

Ruby has long, curly blond hair. Smart, ambitious, but also humble in a strange way that both touches and impresses him. He watches as people gather around her, drawn by her quiet presence.

An hour into the second set, she makes eye contact and mouths the word *wait*. Sometimes she catches him, sometimes she doesn't. Ren nods slightly and takes another sip of beer. Twenty minutes later, after a steady escalating of volume, the set ends, and the woman stands up from behind the piano, bows and walks straight to where Ren is standing. "Drinking from glass, I see," she says. "Classy." She hesitates for a moment longer and then leans forward into Ren, hugging him hard around the chest.

"They didn't have any white wine spritzers," he says, smiling for the first time in weeks. "Your mom?"

"Good," Ruby says, smiling back. "Very good. You need to come by more often." She has huge brown eyes that dominate her face. Intelligent, aware eyes.

"New number," he says. "You ready?"

"Go," she says.

"7685551156."

"Got it?"

"Of course. I'm not a retard, Ren," she says. She takes a sip of his beer and then recites the number backward.

"Anything else going on?" Ren asks, his tone turning serious.

"It's Manhattan, Ren. There's always something going on."

He looks down at her face. Even leaning on the bar at an angle, he's still a foot taller than her.

"No hang-ups, no follows, no serious stalkers, no one shooting at me. Anyone ever tell you you're paranoid?"

"Julia Kenner?"

"I heard the name, but I don't really know her. Why do you ask?"

"I served with her father. Said she had some trouble. Asked me to look in."

"Is it ever just social with you?"

Ren shrugs. "He thinks she's in trouble. And I've never known him to be wrong."

"You big-ass stupid grunts are all the same," she says, faking a small smile.

"Yes," he says. "Recognize anyone odd hanging around or asking about her recently?"

"No. I'd barely even recognize her. Different circles. I was never really accepted into the 'OMG' set," she says, taking another pull from his beer.

When he doesn't respond, her smile fades instantly. "What is it, Ren? I know that face."

"Just be careful," he says. "I mean it."

"Are you staying in the city? Want to get a coffee?"

"Something I've got to do," he says. "Sorry."

REN: coming 2015

"I miss you," she says, looking down at the counter of the bar.

"Be careful, Ruby. Remember that number."

Ren kisses her on the cheek and leaves the room, saying the ritual goodbye in his mind. Avoiding the small tears forming in the corner of her big eyes. Only truly sad people can sing that well.

He exits the bar and walks directly to a blue sedan idling across the street, half a block away. He'd spotted the car on the way in and watched from inside the bar, hoping it was just a coincidence. But Ren doesn't believe in coincidences. Or luck. Or accidents. Whatever happens is always someone's fault, and when it comes to his family, he is that someone.

He enters the sedan through the back door, sitting on the edge of the seat and pushing his matte black Desert Eagle .50 automatic against the back of the head occupying the passenger seat.

"Tell me why I shouldn't shoot your partner in the back of the head, Agent Wilson," he says, staring at her in the rearview mirror. "Make it quick."

"We have a job for you, Ren," she says, making sure to keep her hands on the steering wheel.

"You're following my niece, Ms. Wilson."

"No," the man in the passenger seat says. "We're intercepting—"

Ren clubs the man in the back of his head with the butt of the heavy pistol before he completes the sentence. The man slumps forward and goes limp against the dashboard as Ren swivels the gun toward the driver's seat.

"You know where I live, Wilson, and yet you come here."

"Closer to the airport," she says, staring at his face in the mirror.

"Bullshit, Victoria," he says. "What's the job?"

Wilson looks over at her partner slumped against the dashboard in the passenger seat. "Daughter of an H.S. resource, someone you know," she says, having decided on the flight to tell at least part of the truth.

"You don't make personal contact for a placement."

"It's not a placement," Wilson says, staring at the mirror and keeping her body upright and still. "It's a retrieval."

"I don't do that," he says, the gun pressed against the back of her neck. "You know better."

"Following orders, Ren. Washington has changed. You know that."

Ren settles back into his seat, keeping the gun aimed at the back of her head. "Your orders can get you killed, Victoria. Learned that well enough on my first tour. Taught it to others on my third.

"What do you want with Ruby?"

"Knows the vic, possibly."

"Drive, Wilson. You can keep your two guns, but understand: I'm faster. And you threatened my family just by coming here. The bullet will enter your brain and exit your forehead before the message even reaches your fingers. Clear?"

REN: coming 2015

Wilson nods and starts the engine. "Where to?" she asks, putting the car in drive.

"East," he says.

When they reach the river, he directs her to handcuff her partner to the wheel and retrieves his two guns, cell phone, keys and handcuff spare that all feds carry, often in creative places.

"He'll be out for hours," she says.

Ren opens the car door and turns his body toward the street, keeping the gun centered on Wilson's head. "Get out of the car, slowly, with your hands high in the air. Walk in front of me to the rear of the car. Leave your gun, phone and wallet in the trunk."

"Yes, sir," she says under her breath as she walks around to the back of the car and deposits her equipment in the trunk. Ren adds the other agent's guns, wallet, phone and keys.

FOUR

East River Promenade, Manhattan, N.Y. 2 A.M.

"Talk."

Wilson turns around and leans her back against the railing. "Gun in New York City," she says, staring at the weapon in Ren's hand. "Risky, even for you."

"I won't ask again, Victoria."

"Jack Kenner."

"What about him?"

"You served with him, two tours. We know he contacted you."

"You also know that I broke his arm. That he testified against me. That I don't do retrievals. That I don't do military. And that Homeland Security is a thousand angry teenagers with advanced weaponry."

"Kenner's daughter, kidnapped 12 hours ago. Goes to the same college as Ruby," Wilson says. "We can't ignore the coincidence."

"Casual contact. I already relayed this information to Kenner," Ren says, lowering the gun as a jogger passes by. Only in New York, he thinks to himself, do people jog in the middle of the night.

"You spoke with him?" she asks.

"I met with him," Ren says, raising the gun again. "As I said, coincidence. Ruby's never even spoken with his daughter. Kenner's a piece of shit, lied to me to force me to help."

"Today?" Wilson asks, confused.

"Three days ago."

"Before the kidnapping, then."

"There is no kidnapping, Wilson."

"Of course there's a kidnapping. We've had Kenner under a microscope since the beginning," Wilson says, annoyed with his cryptic answers.

REN: coming 2015

"Not from the beginning. From when the locals called you in. Think, Wilson," Ren says, finally lowering the gun. "They would have been walled off in the house—correction—the compound, five minutes after the threat he came to me for, three days ago. H.S is the biggest gang in the world. Nothing larger than a mosquito would have gotten within a thousand yards of the girl. Yet she's taken from school. Amateur move. Kidnapping's a fake, Wilson."

"You looked into it?"

"I look into everything that affects my family."

"What was the hook?"

"Afghanistan. Said they're circling back to me to find a placement. He was my C.O. Said they couldn't find me, so they got to him. Convincing, but a lie. Designed to involve me from the start."

Wilson turns around slowly, leaning her arms on the river railing and watching a barge pass by. "You don't know that."

"Kenner's a bureaucrat now," Ren says. "Easy enough for him to push this through."

Wilson considers this for a moment.

Ren lowers the gun and leans against the railing beside her. "Every halfway-decent lie makes sense, Victoria."

"You're reaching."

"But you're not sure, are you? The question you need to be asking yourself is not where the girl is, but whether this is an operation, or a father panicking."

Wilson looks sideways, staring at Ren's profile. He might

have been handsome, once, she thinks to herself. "So help on background then."

"No," Ren says. "Not my problem. And it's old. Whatever price he'd pay for anything I'd be a part of, he'd have paid it 12 years ago."

"From you?" she asks, pulling her coat tightly around her chest.

"No," he says.

"They won't stop."

"Who won't stop, Victoria?"

"Us," she says, looking back at the water. "H.S."

"Kenner gave you Ruby?"

Wilson doesn't move, answering slowly. "We never knew much about her, little more than her name, until 12 hours ago," she says. "No reason to dig that deeply."

"Your second lie, Victoria," Ren says, turning to face her. "Who else knows?"

"Besides me? Partner, in the car. Vince Mark, Quantico. Kenner, and whoever he's told."

"Is she in the system?"

"What?" she says, turning toward him.

"Is she in the fucking system!" He yells, his mouth inches from her face.

"I'm sorry, Ren," she says. "Wasn't my call."

"Go fuck yourself, Wilson," Ren says quietly, walking away and leaving her leaning against the railing.

He stops several feet away and turns back toward the

REN: coming 2015

agent. "One more thing, Victoria. If I have to pull Ruby for this, you will all pay a very dear price."

Wilson remains still against the railing as Ren walks away.

ABOUT THE AUTHOR

Photo by Hannah Wulk

Brett Garcia Rose is a writer, software entrepreneur, and former animal rights soldier and stutterer. His work has been published in *Sunday Newsday Magazine*, *The Barcelona Review*, *Opium*, *Rose and Thorn*, *The Battered Suitcase*, *Fiction Attic*, *Paraphilia* and other literary magazines and anthologies. His short stories have won the Fiction Attic's Short Memoir Award and been nominated for the Million Writer's Award, Best of the Net, The Pushcart Prize, The Lascaux Prize for Short Fiction, and Opium's Bookmark competition.

Rose travels extensively, but calls New York City home.

WWW.BRETTGARCIAROSE.COM

Made in the USA
Lexington, KY
24 June 2014